THE

Sarah Jane

ADVENTURES

'rom the makers of Doctor Who

BBC CHILDREN'S BOOKS

Published by the Penguin Group
Penguin Books Ltd, 80 Strand, London WC2R 0RL, England
Penguin Group (USA) Inc., 375 Hudson Street, New York, New York 10014, USA
Penguin Group (Australia) Ltd, 250 Camberwell Road, Camberwell, Victoria, 3124, Australia
(a division of Pearson Australia Group Pty Ltd)
Canada, India, New Zealand, South Africa

Published by BBC Children's Books, 2007
Text and design © Children's Character Books, 2007

10 9 8 7 6 5 4 3 2 1

Sarah Jane Adventures © BBC 2007

BBC logo ™ & BBC 1996. Licensed by BBC Worldwide Limited

ISBN 978-1-40590-397-4

Printed in the United Kingdom

THE

Sarah Jane

ADVENTURES

From the makers of Doctor Who

Invasion of the Bane

Written by Terrance Dicks

Based on the script by Russell T Davies
and Gareth Roberts

'I saw amazing things, out there in space. But there's strangeness to be found wherever you turn. Life on Earth can be an adventure, too.

You just have to know where to look.'

SARAH JANE SMITH

Chapter One

Changes

A cartoon Earth, spinning in a cartoon sky. It exploded in a swirl of light, and bright orange letters exploded from the screen.

'BUBBLE SHOCK!'

Three beautiful blonde teenagers, perfect hair, flawless complexions, impossibly white teeth, appeared. They wore bright orange T-shirts, with 'Bubble Shock' written on the front in white lettering, and were surrounded by swirling orange balloons. They clutched white-capped bottles filled with orange liquid.

'Bubble Shock!' they shrieked, grinning madly.

A row of orange bottles appeared and the camera zoomed into a giant close-up...

Maria, smallish, dark, thirteen years old,

shrugged indifferently. 'Bubble Shock' – she'd tried it once when it first came out. It just made her feel sick.

'Oh, she's got the telly working,' said a voice behind her. 'That's the first priority.'

Rolling her eyes at the parental sarcasm, Maria turned. It was moving day, they were in the new house, and her dad, Alan, had just staggered in with yet another cardboard box. He put it down with a sigh of relief, glancing round the big empty room. 'Plenty more boxes,' he said resignedly. 'Do us a favour and find the kettle. I'm parched.'

On the telly ecstatically happy teenagers swigged orange fluid and marched towards the camera brandishing bottles…

'Maria!' shrieked a voice from outside the house.

'Coming!' yelled Maria. She switched off the telly and went outside where two muscular young men in jeans and T-shirts were unloading more boxes from a removal van. They were being supervised, and watched closely, by Maria's mum, Chrissie.

She turned as Maria came out of the house. 'Maria, the cutlery's in the boot, go and fetch it, will you?'

A removal man passed by with yet another box. 'Living room, love?'

'No, the label says "kitchen", can't you read? Don't go through the front door, go round the side. I did say…'

Chrissie hated it when people didn't do as they were told.

Her voice tailed off as her eyes fell on his retreating rear.

'Mind you, not bad…' she said, smirking.

Maria loved her mother very much, but at times she was definitely an embarrassment. 'Mum! Stop fancying the removal men!'

Chrissie grinned. 'Oh, they love it! Besides, they're getting paid. Cutlery, go on!'

Maria groaned and shook her head. She turned and made for the family's old blue banger which was parked on the other side of the road.

A smart green convertible was just pulling into the driveway of the house opposite – a big, grand house set back from the road. The house looked older than Maria's and was much bigger, tall and thin, with turrets and gables. There was something a little spooky about it, thought Maria. A touch of Dracula's castle.

A woman got out of the car and headed for the house. A bit older than Maria's mum, she looked attractive and sophisticated in a stylish purple coat.

N D L 6 K R P 5 V H

'Hiya!' called Maria.

The woman gave her a quick 'Can't-stop-I'm-in-a-rush' smile and hurried on into the house. Maria shrugged, pulled the cutlery box from the car boot, and carried it back to the new house.

Maria watched as the removal men carried the last item, her bed, into her new bedroom at the back of the house. It was a large attic room with a long window and a skylight set in the slanting roof.

'Put it by the window, thanks.'

They plonked down the bed, gave her a friendly nod and trooped downstairs. Maria followed.

Soon she was standing on the front steps with her parents, waving goodbye as the van drove away. 'Thank you, boys!' called her father as the van disappeared.

Her mind a jumble of emotions, Maria looked up at her mother and smiled. The beginning of a new life. She wasn't sure she was going to like it.

Chrissie put her arm round Maria's shoulders and gave her a consoling hug.

'Come on then,' said Alan, and they went inside. They all went into the kitchen and her dad made tea.

Surrounded by boxes, they stood sipping the

tea. Just like a normal happy family, thought Maria. If only…

There was a moment of awkward silence. Alan looked round the cluttered kitchen and gave one of his optimistic grins. 'All done,' he said, with determined cheerfulness. 'Congratulations. Our new home!'

Maria's mother returned the smile, very briefly, and then looked at her watch.

'Ooh, look at me, it's nearly six. I'd better be off.'

A knot formed in the pit of Maria's stomach. Another parting. The latest of many with many more to come. But she was getting used to it by now, and managed to put a fairly brave face on things.

'Can't you stay for tea, Mum?'

Chrissie, as usual, was totally focussed on her own affairs.

'I'd love to, but Ivan's making me dinner back home.'

This is where the happy family picture falls apart, thought Maria.

Her parents had recently split up. She still wasn't used to it, didn't think she ever would be. The divorce had been what they call 'amicable' – largely because her dad was so easy-going. It didn't make it any less painful for Maria. Like many children of divorce, she had a vague feeling it was all her fault.

She looked at her dad. An average-looking man in jeans and stripy T-shirt. A nice ordinary man. Too ordinary for Chrissie, who wanted glamour and excitement – now being provided by Ivan, some sort of City banker.

Chrissie looked at her daughter's sad face. She produced an encouraging smile. 'You're gonna love it here, sweetheart, I promise.'

'I liked the old house,' muttered Maria.

'Your mother wanted the money,' said Alan quietly.

Chrissie shot him one of her looks. 'Now, don't start.' She turned to Maria. 'It's a much better catchment area, you'll be at a better school. They were holding you back in that old place. The local kids you were mixing with…'

'They were my friends.'

'Well, you'll get a better catchment of friends,' said Chrissie brightly, and gave her a quick kiss. 'You'll settle in, don't worry.' She gave Alan a token peck on the cheek. 'And you. Good luck. You still can't make a decent cup of tea,' she added, putting him down as usual.

She bustled out. Alan gave Maria a resigned

look. He jerked his head towards the door and they followed her outside.

Chrissie paused for a moment on the doorstep. 'Oh, and Alan, I nearly forgot, can you give me that cheque?'

'Dunno where my chequebook is. Buried in a box somewhere.'

'That's all right, post it,' said Chrissie. Her voice became a little sharper. 'First thing tomorrow if you could.'

'Sure,' said Alan.

Chrissie gave Maria a final wave. 'Angel, bye bye. Big kiss!'

She got in her car, a smart new red saloon, and drove away. Maria watched her go.

Alan turned to Maria and gave her a hug. He kissed the top of her head.

'You and me, eh?'

Maria gave him a rueful smile and waved at her mother's departing car as it vanished around the corner.

Maria was in her new bedroom unpacking with the TV on low in the background.

'Bubble Shock, for maximum performance,' the teenagers on the TV chanted. 'No sugar, no additives, no concentrates! Bubble Shock! Contains Bane! Bubble Shock!' flashed in giant letters across the screen.

Maria was taking framed photographs from a box and arranging them on a shelf. The last photo showed the three of them, Alan, Chrissie and Maria, on holiday, only last year. They were all smiling. Those were the days, she thought.

Maria switched off the TV and climbed into bed. She took a battered teddy from her pillow and cuddled it as she slid under the covers. A bit childish for thirteen, maybe, but she didn't care.

She reached out and switched off the bedside lamp and lay staring into the darkness. Her mind was a mad jumble of confused thoughts and feelings and she thought she'd never get to sleep. But it had been a long and tiring day. Eventually sheer exhaustion overcame her and she drifted off…

She had no way of knowing that these few moments marked the end of her ordinary, everyday life.

Maria didn't really register the multi-coloured lights that flashed across the sky, and shone through her windows. It was the music that woke her. Weird ethereal music, like nothing she'd ever heard before.

Maria looked at her bedside clock. It said 2.37.

She got out of bed, took her big blue dressing gown from the hook behind the door and put it on, shoved her feet into slippers and hurried downstairs. The house was dark and spooky and silent – except for the music. It grew louder as she neared the glass-fronted front door and she could see soft coloured lights through the glass.

She opened the door and looked out. More multi-coloured lights played across the front of the spooky old house opposite, moving along the branches of the trees. The seductive song rose and fell and seemed to be calling to her. It was irresistible... Maria dashed across the road.

The sound seemed to be coming from the side of the house. Maria followed it, opened a gate and crept down a tree-shadowed path. The music and the lights seemed to be coming from an enclosed side-garden. Maria crept closer, and peered through the bushes. Her eyes widened in sheer disbelief.

The woman she'd seen going into the house earlier was standing in the garden with a glowing heart-shaped device in her hand. In front of her hovered a shape – an apparition. An impossible, unbelievably beautiful shape.

It was a woman made of clouds and light,

incredibly tall, with wild streaming hair. Transparent and somehow solid at the same time, she was dressed in flowing robes and surrounded by an aura of multi-coloured lights. And she was singing, singing the ethereally beautiful song. As she sang she seemed to dance in the air, revolving around the woman looking up at her.

The woman, the one Maria had seen before, was turning too, so that they seemed to be performing a kind of ritual dance…

So strange and beautiful was the spectacle that Maria found herself smiling.

The woman stopped turning and stood gazing up at the strange alien being. Like Maria, she was not frightened but delighted and fascinated. She was smiling, too. She held up the glowing heart-shaped device and although she didn't speak, Maria knew that in some strange way the two were *communicating*.

The song rose and fell and faded away.

The woman held up the glowing disc in what seemed like a gesture of farewell. The alien quickly rose into the sky and soared into the night, leaving a fiery trail like a rocket as she streaked away and disappeared amongst the stars.

The woman watched it for a moment, her face

filled with delight. She turned and went back into the house.

All at once, Maria realised the strangeness, the sheer impossibility of what she'd seen and awe changed to panic. She turned and ran quickly from the garden, shot across the road and vanished into her new house, slamming the door behind her.

Chapter Two

A visit from Kelsey

Maria sat absent-mindedly drinking tea and eating toast in the new kitchen. Her head was still full of the events of last night. Had she really seen a beautiful alien woman, hovering in the air, and disappearing back into space? And how did the woman who lived in the house come into it? Was she an alien, too?

Her father was precariously balanced on the back of the sofa, adjusting curtain rings on the rail above the window. On the screen of the kitchen telly, teenagers once again danced and skateboarded and

H 4 T R F G 8 N D 1 S W O B X O 3 T R 2 U F S 7 K

chanted in praise of 'Bubble Shock!'

Maria looked up at her father. 'How would you know if you were going mad?'

Her father tightened a screw. 'Ask your mother, she's the expert.'

'I'll tell her you said that!' threatened Maria, and her father grinned. 'But seriously,' she went on. 'What if you see something that can't be happening, only it is happening, only it can't be?'

Her dad jumped down from the sofa and gave her a puzzled frown. Before he could work out an answer, the front doorbell rang, letting him off the hook.

He nodded towards the front door. 'Go and ask them!'

'That's our first visitors,' said Maria.

'If it's Angela Jolie, tell her I'm not interested,' said Alan. He nodded towards the front door. 'Go on.'

Maria went out into the hall and opened the front door.

A girl of about her own age stood on the doorstep. Her hair stuck out in twin plaits, and she wore a bright red puffer jacket and hot pink hoodie. She was drinking from a bottle of Bubble Shock and was studying Maria critically.

'You moved in yesterday, right?'

'Yeah.'

'I saw you.' Apparently deciding Maria passed muster, the girl gave her a beaming grin that lit up her whole face. 'I'm Kelsey. Hiya.'

'Hiya. I'm Maria.'

'You got broadband?'

'Yeah.'

'Brilliant!' Brushing Maria aside, Kelsey marched into the house.

Bemused, Maria followed.

Kelsey marched into the box-cluttered living room, switched on the telly and studied the set-up menu. 'You haven't got the music channels! What's the point if you haven't got music channels?'

For some reason, Maria felt guilty. 'Dad says it costs.'

'Nag him,' advised Kelsey. 'You'll be dead in school if you haven't got music channels.' She held out the bottle of Bubble Shock. 'Want some of this?'

'No thanks, don't like it.'

'I love it,' said Kelsey, taking another swig. 'Do you want to come into town?'

'Haven't got any money.'

'That's all right, we'll get the Bubble Shock bus. It's free, every half hour. Come on, get your stuff.'

'There's a free bus?'

Kelsey brandished the Bubble Shock bottle. 'Yeah, it takes you to the Bubble Shock factory. You go on a tour, get free samples and things, then we all go down the precinct. Come on! I'll show you Darren, he works in the bike shop, he's over buff!'

Kelsey marched off and Maria, slightly stunned by the force of her overpowering personality, followed meekly.

'Dad, I'm going out!' she shouted.

They had just left the house when her father appeared on the front doorstep.

'Heading off without me?'

'We're going into town,' explained Maria.

'Without a proper goodbye?'

Maria writhed. 'Oh Daa-aad…'

With a mock-stern expression, Alan pointed to his cheek and leaned forward.

Maria walked back to him and gave him a kiss on the cheek.

She looked guiltily at Kelsey, who shook her head. 'I'm so shamed for you!'

'Who's your friend?' asked Alan.

'This is Kelsey.'

Kelsey gave Alan a challenging stare. 'Did they tell you? About the people that used to live here?'

'No, what happened?'

'They went mad,' said Kelsey with relish. 'Ran away, screaming. My mum's friend, Kath Pontin, she lives down there, said the bloke kept going on about aliens. From outer space!'

'What sort of aliens?' asked Maria.

'Oh, like it's real, shut up!' said Kelsey dismissively. 'Come on, we're gonna miss the bus.' She set off down the road.

Maria turned to follow her and saw their neighbour, the woman she'd seen entertaining an alien, on the other side of the road. She posted a letter in the letter box and turned back towards her house.

The memory of last night made Maria nervous, but she felt she had to make contact. She hurried across the road. 'Hello, we just moved in opposite. I'm Maria Jackson'.

'Hello,' said the woman and carried on walking.

Alan came hurrying across the road. 'Hi! Hello there, nice to meet you. I'm Alan, Alan Jackson.'

The woman stopped, turned and surveyed Alan without enthusiasm.

'Hi.' She paused, then added, 'I hope you're not going to make too much noise. It's just I work from home and I don't like to be disturbed.' She went on her way.

'Okay,' said Alan, equally coolly. 'Nice to be made welcome.'

The woman stopped again and turned, as if she recognised and regretted her rudeness. She gave Alan an unexpectedly charming smile. 'Sorry! Sarah Jane Smith.'

Kelsey came up and muttered in Martha's ear. 'Local lunatic!' She tried to bustle her away. 'See ya, then.'

'Where are you going exactly?' said Alan.

'Bubble Shock factory,' said Maria.

'Free bus,' explained Kelsey, and the two girls hurried off down the street.

'Anyway, I'm sure we'll get on just fine,' said Alan.

Sarah Jane wasn't listening. She was staring after the two girls in fascination.

'It's only me and Maria now,' Alan went on, feeling he needed to talk. 'Making a new start of it. Bit of a divorce and that.' He grinned ruefully. 'Don't worry, it's all been sorted, no shouting!'

Sarah Jane made no reply. She was still staring after the departing girls.

Determined to be neighbourly, Alan pressed on. 'So, what sort of work do you do?'

Sarah Jane turned and stared at him as if she'd

just realised he was there. Then, without a word, she turned, and sprinted for the car parked in her driveway.

Alan stared after her, bemused. 'Really?' he muttered. 'Must be fascinating.' He leaped aside as the green convertible shot out of the driveway and disappeared down the road. Shaking his head – just his luck to get a nutty neighbour – Alan turned and went back into the house.

Maria and Kelsey were walking down a nearby street, towards a bus stop. Kelsey was stabbing at the buttons on Maria's mobile phone. She handed it back. 'There you go, you've got my number. *Don't* give it to anyone in Year Eight.'

The green convertible sped past and Kelsey went on, 'That's the mad woman, always racing about.'

'She's a bit glamorous though,' said Maria. 'What does she do?'

They'd reached the bus stop with a poster practically shouting: 'Bubble Shock! Drink it!' and a picture of the usual delirious teenagers clutching orange bottles.

Kelsey shrugged. 'Journalist or something. My mum's friend Kath Pontin says she never has anyone round. No mates, nothing. But she's always going out in the middle of the night. Never talks to anyone.' Kelsey lowered her voice. 'And this guy Sakkim in Year Eleven, he says he once saw her in the park by the station. She was talking to this big crystal thing and it *moved…*'

Maria's mind flashed back to the incredible scene last night.

'What, like a monster or something?'

Before Kelsey could answer, a bus swung round the corner. It was bright orange, plastered with slogans. 'Bubble Shock! Contains Bane. Drink it!' in giant letters. It was blaring out the irritating Bubble Shock jingle that always seemed to be on the telly.

Kelsey beamed with delight. 'Here it is!'

Her joy was infectious, and Maria found herself grinning, too. They piled on to the bus.

Maria saw that there were already about twenty people on board. Mostly teenagers, but some adults and a few little kids as well. On the bus wall, screens showed Bubble Shock commercials in an continuous loop.

A huge tray just inside the door was piled high with orange bottles. Kelsey took one, brandished it triumphantly, and plonked herself down in an empty double seat. Maria took the seat in front and swung round to face her.

She looked at the crowd of Bubble Shock enthusiasts all around her and shook her head. 'I don't get how this Bubble Shock stuff's supposed to work.'

'I don't care,' said Kelsey simply. 'It just makes you feel all wide awake and stuff. And it tastes fab.'

'I think it tastes disgusting,' said Maria.

'You're one of the two per cent then,' said Kelsey resignedly. 'It doesn't work on two per cent of people. That's a fact. Anyway, it's organic!'

She seemed to think that this was the clincher.

Maria took the bottle from her and studied it. 'So that makes it all right? Just the magic word "organic"?'

Kelsey snatched the bottle back. 'Well, it's natural. And that's good.'

She looked so comically defiant that Maria burst out laughing, and Kelsey laughed too.

'Drink it! Drink it!' shrieked the commercial.

The bus drove past yet another Bubble Shock poster. Out of nowhere, a green convertible slid out of a side street and followed.

Behind the wheel, Sarah Jane fixed her eyes on the large orange shape ahead. The bus drove on, stopping now and again to pick up more passengers. Leaving the suburbs behind, the bus led her to an ultra-modern factory building in a quiet lane on the edge of town. It was protected by a high metal fence and vast iron gates.

Inside the bus, a cheer went up as the factory came in sight.

Maria studied the factory – a linked cluster of gleaming industrial buildings, some squat, some long and thin, and some cylindrical towers. The whole place seemed to be constructed of corrugated metal and plastic. Huge metal pipes ran along the outer walls, and there were mysterious vents and turrets everywhere. The factory looked ultra-modern and sinister.

Kelsey greeted it with delight. 'There it is!' she shouted. 'Bubble Shock!'

The huge gates swung open and the bus passed through. The gates began to close behind them.

In the green convertible, Sarah Jane's eyes widened. On impulse, she put her foot down and the car shot through the rapidly shrinking gap, with inches to spare.

The gates clanged shut behind her.

She was in! A thought flashed through Sarah Jane's mind. How was she going to get out?

Chapter Three

The Bane
tour

Sarah Jane parked behind a side building and got out of the car. She looked around her. For the moment at least, there seemed to be nobody in sight. Flattening herself against the corrugated metal wall she peered around the corner.

Straight ahead was the big orange tour bus. It was parked beside the visitor's entrance. There was an orange panel over the door, bearing the words 'WELCOME TO BUBBLE SHOCK!' in giant letters. Orange balloons hung over the doorway and the entrance was flanked by guards in orange-overalls and white-helmets. The passengers from the bus were already filing inside, followed closely by the guards.

Sarah Jane considered tagging on to the tour, but rejected the idea immediately. Too public, she thought, and too well-supervised. It was unlikely that whoever ran the factory would allow visitors to wander around at will – which was what Sarah Jane wanted to do. She must find some other way in.

She looked at her wristwatch. It was a man's watch, a rather old-fashioned affair with an oblong face. She flicked open the face and it lifted like a lid, revealing an electronic screen filled with flickering data. She studied it for a moment then snapped it closed.

'I knew it!' said Sarah Jane.

Maria followed Kelsey and the others into the building, along a short corridor and through a metal door, which led into a metal-walled ante-room. Straight ahead was a metal arch, the kind you see in airports.

An orange-overalled guard stood beside it at a keyboard console. A handsome young man clutching a clipboard appeared.

'That's Davey, the chief tour guide,' whispered Kelsey. 'He's well buff!'

Maria nodded. Davey was handsome enough,

she thought, but there was something cold and cruel about him. Something remote and detached, almost alien…

'Right, welcome to the Bubble Shock experience,' said Davey, in the bored voice of a man who'd said the same thing hundreds of times before. 'If you could all step through the archway, one by one, thank you. Just a security scan.' Two boys at the head of the line hurried forward, each trying to get through first. 'One at a time, thank you,' said Davey wearily.

The boys went through in single file. There was a flash of light as each passed through the archway and the rest of the crowd followed.

Maria held Kelsey back, letting the others move past them. There was something very disturbing about all these exaggerated precautions.

Maria gave Kelsey a sceptical look. 'A security scan in a pop factory?'

'People want to steal the recipe!' said Kelsey. They were last in the queue now. Kelsey moved to the archway and went through, triggering the flash. 'Come on, it doesn't hurt.'

Bracing herself, Maria stepped through the archway…

In the Data Room in the factory, Maria's image appeared frozen on a screen. It was surrounded by flashing data. All around other screens flared and flickered, recording and transmitting more data.

A bored technician looked up from his console.

'Last of today's first lot going through now. Transmitting data to the Archetype in five, four, three…'

In a shadowy area at the back of the laboratory, a woman stood over a long table, rather like a mortician's slab. A slender, smallish shape lay on the table, covered by a white sheet. A variety of medical wires and tubes ran under the sheet, attached to the body below.

'…two, one – transmit!' said the technician.

There was a crackle of energy and the body under the sheet twitched and shuddered. Lights flashed on the surrounding screen and consoles.

The woman stepped forward into the light. She was tall and stately, impressive in a black silk dress. She wore jet-black earrings and an emerald ring. There was a blazing emerald pendant at her throat. Beautiful, with icy blue eyes, she had an air of tremendous authority. Like Davey the tour guide, there was something cruel and inhuman about her good looks.

Her name – or rather the name she had chosen to use – was Mrs Wormwood.

'Is it working?' asked the technician.

'Oh yes,' said Mrs Wormwood softly. 'He's almost fully mature.' She lifted a corner of the sheet and reverently touched the still young face beneath. 'I would even say, perfect! Mother *will* be pleased…'

Sarah Jane was edging her way round the metal buildings, careful to hide when she caught sight of the occasional orange-clad worker. There seemed to be very few of them. She guessed the factory must be largely automated.

She came to a metal door with a massive lock. A sign above it read, 'Switch Room'. She took what looked like a lipstick from her pocket, uncapped it and held it up to the door. The end of the lipstick glowed red and there was a crackle of energy as the door unlocked.

At this point, Sarah Jane's plans suffered an unfortunate set-back.

She pulled the door open and found herself facing two guards. Burly and thuggish, they stared down at her.

'Oops!' said Sarah Jane.

Mrs Wormwood put a hand to her ear as a voice crackled into the discreet com-unit earpiece hidden by her hair. It was Lesley, her secretary.

'Mrs Wormwood? We have an intruder.'

'Well, dispose of him.'

'It's a human female. She says her name is Sarah Jane Smith.'

Mrs Wormwood seemed delighted. 'Does she indeed? Then bring her to my office. And make her welcome.' She smiled an unpleasant smile. 'This should be fun.'

Davey, the tour guide, marched the little group along a metal corridor, through another security door and down a short flight of steps into the main factory area. It was filled with complex and mysterious machinery. Giant vats bubbled and hissed and gave out wafts of Bubble Shock-scented vapour. Kelsey sniffed it luxuriously.

Maria found it made her feel a little sick. No doubt about it, she was one of the two per cent. She gazed around the factory floor, impressed despite herself.

'It's huge…'

'Seen it loads of times,' said Kelsey loftily.

Davey addressed the group. 'Just a reminder… if

you could turn your mobile phones off? That means all of you. We've got sensitive equipment in here and the signal can interfere with the machinery. So, mobile phones off, thank you.'

Most of the group started fishing out mobile phones and switching them off. Maria and Kelsey did the same.

Maria looked at her phone. 'What's a mobile gonna do, make the bubbles go flat?'

Davey must have had acute hearing because he snapped, 'That's enough lip at the back! Just do it. Thank you.'

Obediently, Kelsey and Maria switched off their phones.

'He's a bit rude,' muttered Maria.

Kelsey gazed at the guide. 'I don't care. He's a total muffin!'

'Okay, everyone,' said the total muffin in the same flat, bored voice. 'This, as you can see, is the main production area. And before we go any further, I'd like to offer you more free samples. Help yourselves!'

He indicated a nearby trolley holding an open crate piled high with bottles of Bubble Shock, and droned on with his tour guide patter. 'Bubble Shock revitalises your taste buds, gives you energy morning, noon and night. Only Bubble Shock contains Bane! Keep moving now, that's it, don't touch anything, move along now, free Bubble Shock…'

The tour group filed past, grabbing bottles, with some people grabbing several.

Maria just walked past – and Davey noticed. He pushed the trolley towards her. 'Oi, you! No Bubble Shock?'

She shook her head. 'No, thanks. I'm one of the two per cent with the wrong taste buds.'

Davey smiled coldly. 'Don't worry, we're working on it. Soon we'll have everyone drinking Bane. The whole world…' He took a bottle from the crate and tossed it to her.

Maria stared defiantly at him and tossed the bottle back in the crate. 'I'd rather have a cup of tea.'

Sarah Jane was sitting in the guest chair in front of Mrs Wormwood's enormous desk, trying to look a lot less apprehensive that she felt. She had already decided on her story. All she had to do now was to keep calm and bluff through it.

Mrs Wormwood's secretary, tall and as elegant as her mistress, placed a cup of tea on the glass desk-top in front of Sarah Jane and moved away.

'Thank you,' said Sarah Jane. 'That's very kind.'

Sitting on the other side of the desk, Mrs Wormwood smiled and said, 'Think of yourself as our guest.'

Somehow she made the polite words sound like a threat.

Sarah Jane smiled back and glanced around the office. It was an enormous ultra-modern affair designed in glass and steel with huge picture windows. Judging by its size, Mrs Wormwood must be very important indeed.

She launched into her story. 'I wasn't breaking in. I was just trying to reach someone in charge. I phoned about a hundred times but no one would talk to me.'

'Oh, I've seen the list,' said Mrs Wormwood. 'Letters, phone calls, e-mails…Miss Sarah Jane Smith certainly makes her presence felt!'

Doing her best to look every inch the determined, professional, investigative journalist, Sarah Jane produced a notebook. 'Do you mind if I take notes?'

Mrs Wormwood produced a smile of saccharin sweetness. 'Not at all. Since you've been so bold, let's make this an official interview.'

Sarah Jane opened her notebook. 'And it's…Mrs Wormwood?'

'That is correct.'

'As a matter of fact it's in the Bible, Wormwood,' said Sarah Jane brightly. 'The Book of Revelations. At the end of the world, it describes a star, falling to Earth and poisoning the waters. A star called Wormwood.'

'Fascinating,' said Mrs Wormwood uninterestedly. 'Shall we move on to business?'

Sarah Jane changed tack. 'I've got contacts in the City,' she said. 'They say it was like this company dropped in from nowhere. Normally, it takes years of tests to get approval to market a new foodstuff. You got it in two weeks.'

Mrs Wormwood assumed an expression of virtuous innocence.

'All we're doing is satisfying a need.'

'Which is?'

Mrs Wormwood's eyes gleamed. 'The people are hungry, Miss Smith. Hungry for new food, new drink, new tastes. All the Western world does is eat!' Her voice rose higher quickening with excitement. 'All day, every day, eating, they gorge and feast and chew and bite, all sweet and hot and cold and sticky. Food and drink, just food and drink, that's the human race. They devour! Who are we to deny them?'

'So you invented Bane?'

Mrs Wormwood rose. 'Oh, the Bane inside Bubble Shock isn't new, Miss Smith. It's very, very old. Come and see.'

She moved over to a giant wall screen, and Sarah Jane followed.

On the screen deliriously happy teenagers sung and danced and skateboarded and turned somersaults, all clutching little orange bottles.

'Bane!' screamed the soundtrack. 'The brand new taste for a new generation. Bane gives you life, gives you energy, gives you get-up-and-go!'

'For all the hype, Bane is totally natural,' said Mrs Wormwood persuasively. 'One hundred per cent organic.'

'Yes,' said Sarah Jane. 'But organic what?'

Mrs Wormwood laughed. 'Now don't be silly, I can hardly give away our recipe.'

'I checked with some scientists I know…' began Sarah Jane.

Mrs Wormwood sighed. 'Your social circle sounds fascinating.'

'They tried to analyse a bottle of Bubble Shock – '

'Oh, what good is analysis?' said Mrs Wormwood

impatiently. 'That's just chemicals and sweeteners and E-numbers. The test of a drink is in the tasting. Have you tried it?'

'Oh no. Definitely not!

'But you must. Lesley!'

Her secretary appeared, holding a bottle of Bubble Shock. She handed it to Mrs Wormwood, who tried to hand it to Sarah Jane.

Sarah Jane shook her head. 'No, really. Thanks, I'm fine.'

'But I insist!' Mrs Wormwood twisted the cap, and there was a sinister little hiss of gas. She held out the bottle. 'A good journalist should submit to the complete experience.' Her voice became stern, commanding. She stared hypnotically at Sarah Jane. 'Drink Bubble Shock, Miss Smith. Drink deep!'

'Mrs Wormwood,' said Sarah Jane, 'I'd rather die.'

Somehow Sarah Jane sensed that Mrs Wormwood would just love to take her up on the offer. Her calm gaze met and held Mrs Wormwood's fierce glare.

Then Mrs Wormwood forced a smile. 'Well, we can't have that, can we?'

There was a burst of music from the wall screen.

'Bane has received ringing endorsements!'

On the screen the scene changed to the Blue Peter

studio. Two attractive presenters, a young man and a pretty girl, clutched bottles of Bubble Shock.

'Now I know we're not supposed to advertise,' said the young man. 'But we have to make an exception for this!' He held up the bottle.

'You've got to try Bubble Shock,' said the girl. 'It's just delicious!'

They both brandished their bottles. 'Drink it!'

Good grief, thought Sarah Jane, this is serious. They've even corrupted Blue Peter!

Mrs Wormwood clicked off the screen, stalked back to her desk and sat down.

Sarah Jane followed. 'Those scientists I was talking about, the ones who tried to analyse Bubble Shock – they said that Bane behaves very oddly when they try to test it. As if it's resisting the analysis.' She looked hard at Mrs Wormwood. 'And nothing could do that. At least…nothing on Earth.'

'What exactly are you suggesting?' asked Mrs Wormwood coolly. 'That Bane originated in outer space?'

'Of course not,' said Sarah Jane. 'That would be ridiculous.'

'Wouldn't it though?' said Mrs Wormwood – and smiled her terrible smile.

Chapter Four

Hunted

Davey's little tour group had arrived at a giant metal vat surrounded by clouds of steam. Above it, an enormous funnel swooped down from the factory roof high above. Somehow, Maria sensed that this was the central point of the entire process.

Davey certainly seemed to think so. His face rapt, he gazed reverently up at the giant funnel. 'So the pure spring water and fresh fruit juice ends up here, where Bane is added. And from here it's bottled, all quality controlled, and packed up ready to be distributed all over the British Isles…'

For the first time, there was real passion in his voice and Maria couldn't help being impressed. Kelsey, on the other hand, a veteran of many visits, was thoroughly bored.

'Listen,' she whispered. 'We'll be done in twenty minutes. I'll go and phone Suki, she can meet us at WH Smith's in the precinct.'

Maria gave her a worried look. 'You're not supposed to use your phone.'

Kelsey sniffed. 'What are you, a Girl Guide?'

Maria glanced at Davey, who was still going on about the virtues of Bane.

'He'll take it off you.'

'Well, he's not gonna see, is he?' said Kelsey triumphantly. She grinned. 'Suki's dead rich.'

As Davey moved over to a display stand piled high with Bubble Shock bottles, Kelsey slipped quietly away.

'Every bottle is dated and stamped with the Bubble Shock seal of approval,' Davey was saying. 'Making it the nation's number one!'

Worried that he'd notice that Kelsey was missing, Maria tried a quick distraction. 'This Bane stuff, the special ingredient. What is it, exactly?'

Davey paused for a moment, staring at her with shining eyes. His answer was very strange.

'Bane is life,' said Davey, with burning sincerity. 'Bane is all.'

Maria looked thoughtfully at him. There was something very peculiar about Davey…

Mrs Wormwood and Sarah Jane were saying a rather chilly goodbye.

Mrs Wormwood rose and came from behind her desk. 'Go ahead and print your story by all means. But do consider your career. Are you really going to expose all this as some kind of alien plot? You'll be considered insane!'

'I don't care what people think of me,' said Sarah Jane quietly. 'Never have. I just want to find the truth.'

Mrs Wormwood shifted her attack to a more personal level. 'But at such a cost. I take it, Miss Smith, you're single?'

'Yes, I am.'

'No children?'

'No.'

'Such a wasted life,' said Mrs Wormwood sadly. She raised her voice. 'Miss Smith is leaving. Lesley will show you out, Miss Smith.'

The secretary came forward and led Sarah Jane towards the lift.

As she reached it, Sarah Jane turned. 'Oh and by the way – what planet do you come from?'

Mrs Wormwood smiled. 'Nice try!'

The secretary stepped into the lift and Sarah Jane followed. The doors slid closed behind them.

Mrs Wormwood waited for a moment then touched the com-unit in her ear.

'Lesley. Kill her.'

The tall secretary behind her, Sarah Jane stood facing the doors as the lift glided smoothly downwards. Reflected in the mirror-like surface of the doors, she saw the secretary raise her arm for a killer karate-chop…

Without turning, Sarah Jane jabbed backwards in a vicious elbow-strike. It took the secretary in the solar plexus and she collapsed, gasping.

The lift doors opened and Sarah Jane sprang out and ran down the corridor.

Kelsey reached a dark and deserted corridor and decided it would be safe enough. She took out her mobile, flipped it open and scrolled through the long list of her mobile phone mates. 'Sally, Sam, Sammy, Sam2…'

Two guards appeared at the far end of the corridor. Instinctively, Kelsey snapped off the phone and ducked through the nearest door.

She crouched down by the wall beside it, and heard the booted feet of the guards pass by. After a moment she rose and looked around her.

She was in a dark and cavernous metal chamber. A variety of heavy pipes ran up the walls and disappeared into the ceiling high above. The room was filled with strange alien-looking machinery which hissed and gave off fierce puffs of steam.

There was a strange and terrifying atmosphere about the place – something indescribably sinister, like the feeling of a hovering alien presence.

'Blimey,' muttered Kelsey to herself. 'Don't put this on the tour, do they?'

She flipped open her phone, scrolled to 'Suki' and pressed the call button.

'Hiya, Suki…'

All hell broke loose.

The phone emitted a high-pitched piercing shriek which seemed to stab through Kelsey's brain. She yelled and dropped the phone, which slid across the floor.

An alarm blared, deafening her with its howl. All around her the pipes and machinery started to shudder and clank, and steam-jets hissed out furiously.

Kelsey ran for the door but more jets of steam drove her back. From high above there came a terrible slurping roar. Kelsey looked up.

Something horrible was glaring down at her

with one giant eye.

Kelsey screamed…

In the Data Room, sirens howled and machinery shuddered. The sheeted form on the table shook and twitched and its eyes snapped open…

On the main factory floor the alarms were also howling and screaming. Davey herded his little group towards the exit like an angry sheepdog.

'I'm sorry everybody, we have an emergency. That's it, keep moving please…' He grabbed a passing guard by the arm. 'Get them out,' he snarled. 'Get everyone *out!*' He turned and disappeared up a nearby staircase.

From high in the ceiling a huge alien eye gazed down on Kelsey. A giant green tentacle appeared and flailed down towards her.

Kelsey screamed even louder and backed away.

The guard bustled the tour group down a metal staircase.

'Hurry along there please, quick as you can!'

Maria, tailing behind at the back the tour group, suddenly stopped.

'Kelsey,' she muttered. She couldn't just leave her. She turned and ran back up the staircase and along the corridor.

Kelsey backed away into a corner, staring up at the heavy-lidded eye of the alien horror reaching out for her. 'No,' she screamed. 'No, please…'

In her ultra-modern office, which was filled with the scream of alarms, Mrs Wormwood stood with a hand to her com-unit. 'What is it?' she shouted. 'What's happening?'

The lift doors opened and her secretary staggered in, looking very much the worse for wear. 'Mrs Wormwood,' she gasped. 'She escaped.'

'Sarah Jane Smith,' hissed Mrs Wormwood.

Alarms ringing in her ears, Sarah Jane ran along a dark factory corridor.

Not far away, Maria was doing exactly the same thing.

'Kelsey!' she called. 'Kelsey, are you there?'

There was no reply. Just the wail of the sirens. Maria ran on.

In yet another corridor, Davey, followed by two guards, was running towards the source of the disturbance. It seemed to be coming from the heart of the factory – the pipe room, directly below the Nest of the Bane.

Mrs Wormwood marched across the floor of the factory, followed by two guards.

'Find that woman,' she ordered. 'And this time, kill her properly!'

Kelsey crouched, screaming, in a corner of the pipe room, staring hopelessly at the hideous alien creature above her.

Davey burst into the room followed by the guards.

'What have you done?' he shouted furiously.

Kelsey gestured above her. 'Get that thing away from me!'

'She is not a thing!' shouted Davey. 'You are the thing!' He gazed upwards at the monstrosity. 'She is my mother, the mother of us all.'

One of the guards saw Kelsey's mobile on the floor and snatched it up. 'Sir!'

Davey whirled round. 'Well, turn it off!'

The guard threw the phone back on to the floor

and ground it to fragments under his boot-heel. The alarms fell silent.

Indignation overcame Kelsey's fear. 'Oi, that's my phone!'

The thing in the ceiling gave a ferocious howl.

Davey looked upwards. 'There's nothing to be scared of, Mother,' he said soothingly. 'Our precious Bane Mother.'

Maria ran down yet another corridor and emerged into a machine room. Guards ran by on the other side of the room. She ducked behind one of the machines and they passed without seeing her.

It was easier to think now the howling of the alarms had stopped. Maria remembered that Kelsey had given her her mobile phone number. Maria took out her phone, found Kelsey's number and punched the call button. The alarms broke out again in full force, howling and screaming all over the factory. She switched off the phone, but the alarms blared on.

Maria heard booted feet pounding towards her…

Chapter Five

Escape

Maria ducked behind one of the machines as guards ran by on the other side of the room. She crouched down motionless, hardly daring to breathe.

They passed without seeing her. She waited a moment or two and moved on.

'Kelsey?' she called softly. 'Kelsey, are you there?'

In the pipe room, Davey reacted to the renewed alarms in rage.

'Another one!' he snarled.

Kelsey, still paralysed with fear, huddled in her corner, staring up at the alien monstrosity above. Great studded octopus-like tentacles reached down, flailing blindly, as if groping for her…

The room shook as the giant creature above them roared in rage and pain.

It was in the Data Room that the effect of the alarms was most severe.

Consoles shuddered and vibrated and gave off showers of sparks. A technician crouched over the main data console, struggling to close it down.

Suddenly, the console exploded in smoke and flame, hurling the technician across the room.

The sheeted figure on the slab sat up, eyes widening in fear. The sheet fell away revealing the shape of a young boy in a white tunic and shorts.

The boy pulled the breathing-mask from his mouth and began ripping away the wires and sensors that connected him to the surrounding machinery. He swung his legs off the slab and stood up, gazing in astonishment around the smoke-filled room. It seemed as if it was all new to him. Everything was new to him. He had just been born.

Another console exploded. The boy jumped back in alarm. He looked down at the unconscious body of the technician. One overwhelming desire filled his newly conscious mind – the need to escape, to get away from this terrible place.

He fled like a frightened animal through the

open door, and ran in blind panic along the endless corridors.

Maria too was running along yet another darkened corridor. She had given up looking for Kelsey now, and was hunting desperately for an exit.

She turned a corner and ran straight into a white-clad figure.

They both stopped and drew back, staring at each other.

'Um… Hello!' said Maria.

'Um… Hello!' said the boy. He said exactly the same words with exactly the same intonation, like a recording.

Maria studied him curiously. He was oddly dressed, in a white tunic and white shorts. He seemed to be about her own age, perhaps a little younger. Yet, despite his age, there was something blank and innocent about his face. It seemed completely unmarked by experience of any kind.

'Who are you?' asked Maria.

It happened again.

'Who are you?' repeated the boy.

'I'm lost,' said Maria.

'I'm lost,' said the boy.

Maria stared at him in exasperation. Was he

just going to repeat everything she said? Like a parrot?

From somewhere further down the corridor they heard the clang of a metal door opening, excited voices and the pounding of booted feet.

The boy broke into a run, speeding off down the corridor in the opposite direction.

Maria hesitated for a moment, and then ran after him…

Davey gazed adoringly into the great alien eye above him.

'Shroud yourself, Mother,' he whispered. 'We will find the source and destroy it.'

The eye closed and vanished and the great tentacles withdrew.

His com-unit beeped, and he touched his ear. 'Mrs Wormwood? We have the situation under control.'

'Oh, I don't think so,' said Mrs Wormwood's bitter voice.

She was marching into the Data Room, followed by two guards. She stared down at the empty slab.

'The Archetype has escaped. Find him! And for the Bane Mother's sake, turn off these alarms!'

In the factory corridors the sound of the alarms died away.

All through the factory, patrols of guards, thundered up and down the corridors, hunting for the fugitive.

Maria and the boy crouched under a metal staircase as yet another patrol passed by. When they'd gone, Maria smiled at the boy.

'I'm not with them,' she whispered. 'I can help you.'

The boy smiled back – exactly the same smile…

They emerged from hiding. 'We've got to find a safe place to hide,' whispered Maria. She peered around the corner and saw an empty corridor – with a familiar sign on one of the doors.

'Yes!' said Maria. 'Come on.'

She ran through a door marked 'Ladies'. Obediently, the boy followed.

They found themselves in a standard modern toilet. Rows of mirrors and basins on one side, rows of cubicles on the other.

'We'll be safe here for a bit,' said Maria. 'This is the one place men never go.' She smiled apologetically. 'Sorry for dragging you into the ladies.'

'Why do men never go to the ladies?' asked the boy.

Maria looked at him in surprise. It was a weird question – but it was the most original thing he'd said so far.

Like Maria, Sarah Jane was running along dark and smoke-filled corridors, dodging patrols of guards. Now she heard yet another patrol, coming up behind her. There were cries of, 'Find him! He must be found!' and the clump of heavy boots.

Who was 'him' wondered Sarah Jane. Weren't they just after her? Were other fugitives being hunted?

She turned a corner and found herself in an empty corridor with a familiar sign on one of its doors. Sarah Jane smiled to herself. The Ladies – the traditional refuge of every female in trouble. She hurried inside.

Once inside she looked round for a way of escape. She heard movement in a cubicle, flung open the door and found two small figures hiding inside.

She stared at them in amazement. 'What are you doing in here?'

Maria and the boy emerged from their hiding place.

'I could ask you the same!' said Maria.

Sarah Jane looked at the boy. 'Who's he? Why is

he dressed like that?'

'Um. Hello,' said the boy politely. He seemed to think the 'Um' was an essential part of the greeting.

Sarah Jane stared at him. There was something strange about the boy. A sort of – blankness. 'What have they done to you?'

'I knew I had to get away,' said the boy simply.

'That goes for all of us,' said Sarah Jane.

Two patrols of guards, one led by Mrs Wormwood, one led by Davey, came hurrying down the corridor from opposite directions. They stopped, confronting each other.

'You've searched everywhere?' snapped Mrs Wormwood.

Davey nodded. 'It must have left the compound.'

'Impossible!' Mrs Wormwood sniffed the air like a hound on the scent. 'There are still humans here. I can smell them. And one very particular person – still alive.'

She looked up and down the corridor – and fixed on a door. 'Did you search in there?'

'But it's for their females only,' stammered Davey. 'We are males, their culture says we must never go in.'

'Oh, you idiot!' said Mrs Wormwood. Perhaps the Bane introduction course on human customs had been a little *too* thorough, she thought.

Led by Mrs Wormwood, Davey and the guards charged into the Ladies.

Once they were inside, a rapid search revealed that the place was empty.

Mrs Wormwood pointed to a smallish window. It was open.

'Where does that lead?'

'Visitors car park,' said Davey. 'A child could get through there.'

'Or a narrow-hipped female,' said Mrs Wormwood. She turned to the door.

'Quickly – seal the gates!'

Sarah Jane, Maria and the boy ran through the car park to the outbuilding by the gates where Sarah Jane had parked her car.

Sarah Jane shoved the boy into the back seat and turned to Maria. 'Get in!'

Maria hesitated. 'But my friend's in there! Well, I only just met her this morning, but I can't just leave her.'

'The bus is gone,' said Sarah Jane impatiently.

'Maybe she was on the bus. Now get in!'

Maria was in a torment of indecision. She wanted to get away from this awful place. But it seemed all wrong just to leave Kelsey behind.

'I can't…'

There was a whirring and clanking sound and they turned to see that the factory's big metal gates were starting to close. Sarah Jane took her lipstick from her shoulder bag, uncapped it and pointed. There was a low whirring sound, the end of the lipstick glowed red and the still-open gates jammed.

Maria was amazed. 'What is that thing?'

'Sonic lipstick,' said Sarah Jane. 'Now get in!'

There was a commotion behind them, and a rush of footsteps. They turned and saw Mrs Wormwood, Davey and a group of guards surging out of the main factory entrance and running towards them.

That was enough to make up Maria's mind for her. She jumped into the car.

Sarah Jane got behind the wheel, switched on the ignition and gunned the engine.

The car roared through the half-open gates.

Mrs Wormwood held up her hand, halting the pursuit. She had just caught a glimpse of the white-clad figure in the car.

'She's taken the Archetype,' she said with controlled fury. 'Now we can have even more fun. Oh, even more!' She smiled her evil smile.

She turned and marched back to the lift that led to her office.

When she emerged from the lift she saw Kelsey, terrified but defiant, standing in the middle of the room, her small figure dwarfed by two burly guards.

Mrs Wormwood marched towards her.

'Now, let's find out what you know, little girl!'

Chapter Six

Interrogation

S arah Jane's green convertible screeched into her driveway and came to a halt. She jumped out, followed by the white-clad boy. Taking his hand, she led him towards her house.

Maria jumped out after them, still full of unanswered questions.

'But who is he? What was he doing in that factory? What are they doing in there?'

Sarah Jane strode on. 'Just leave it. You go home, Maria, I can handle things from now on.'

'But there's something going on,' insisted Maria. 'I saw you last night!'

Sarah Jane stopped and turned. 'What did you say?'

'She said she saw you last night,' said the boy in his literal way.

'With that thing, in your garden. That... alien.'

Sarah Jane marched up to Maria and glared down at her.

'Now listen to me, Maria. My life is dangerous. And, rule one, I don't put anyone else in danger – especially not a kid.'

'I'm not a kid!'

Sarah Jane ignored her. 'Maria, just go home and watch telly, do whatever you do. Just live your life as normal and forget any of this ever happened. Have you got that? Stay away from me – for your own sake!'

Taking the boy by the arm, she turned and hurried him into the house.

For a moment, Maria stared after them. Then she turned and ran across the road and into the new house, slamming the front door behind her.

As she came into the hall she saw her father unpacking yet another box.

'Hey, I've worked out the oven,' he said cheerfully. 'It was on timer.'

Ignoring him, Maria ran upstairs.

Alan got up and went to the foot of the stairs. 'Maria?' he called.

The only response was the slamming of her bedroom door.

It had been quite a day, thought Alan. No wonder

the poor kid was upset. Best give her a bit of time to get over it.

He went back to his box and carried on unpacking.

Maria grabbed her old teddy and flung herself on her bed. Suddenly it was all too much for her. The divorce, the move, the weird events at the factory – and now Sarah Jane's hostility. She stared into space, her eyes welling with tears.

Mrs Wormwood sat at her desk, Davey standing behind her.

Before her, flanked by guards, stood Kelsey, scared but still stroppy.

'And another thing, I want compensation for that phone. It was brand new last week!' Mrs Wormwood and Davey stared at her. Encouraged, Kelsey nodded towards Davey. 'And for your information, *he* is a prize mentalist. He's got like this big puppet thing living in the roof and he thinks it's his mum.'

'Puppet?' said Mrs Wormwood.

Davey leaned forward. 'She means Mother,' he said, cold anger in his voice.

'Yeah? Well, if that's your mother you should go on Jeremy Kyle,' said Kelsey scornfully.

Mrs Wormwood rose, shaking her head. 'I can't

understand a word she says. She's all noise and ignorance. Whereas, Miss Smith…' She picked up a remote control and moved over to the giant monitor screen. An image of Sarah Jane appeared. 'Miss Smith seems familiar with the concept of alien life. Far too familiar. And look, if we scan her…'

Sarah Jane's image blurred into an infra-red scan.

'An average human,' said Mrs Wormwood. 'Except…'

Suddenly, colours flared, and text scrolled across the bottom of the screen.

'What is it?' asked Davey.

'Residual artron energy,' said Mrs Wormwood. 'Background radiation. A result of travel through the space-time vortex. Some time ago, but it's still there.'

'A space-time traveller?' said Davey unbelievingly.

'So it seems. We must find her.'

Kelsey felt she was being ignored so she decided to chip in.

'She lives on Bannerman Road.'

Mrs Wormwood turned. 'I beg your pardon?'

'Bannerman Road. And she's as loony as you lot.'

'We must retrieve the Archetype,' said Davey. 'And kill the Smith woman.' He smiled. 'I've been dying to kill one of them ever since we arrived.'

Mrs Wormwood looked thoughtfully at Kelsey. 'This one has information. Perhaps we can use her.'

'You can let me go,' said Kelsey indignantly. 'Or I'm phoning the police – and Childline!'

'She's already primed,' said Davey. 'Drinks five bottles of Bubble Shock a day. Her system's full of Bane.'

'Good,' said Mrs Wormwood. She turned to Kelsey. 'I'm going to turn off my image translator. Try not to scream!'

'I never scream,' said Kelsey defiantly.

Mrs Wormwood touched the jewel at her throat. Her form blurred and shimmered and an indescribable alien horror reared up over Kelsey.

She jumped back in horror and the guards grabbed her arms.

The alien horror moved closer.

Kelsey screamed…

There was a tapping on Maria's bedroom door. After a moment the door opened and her dad appeared, clutching a steaming mug of tea.

'Someone said there's a miserable girl who needs a cup of tea. But I couldn't find her, so you'll have to do instead.'

He held out the mug.

Maria was sitting on the side of the bed. She gave him a reluctant smile and took the tea. One thing about her dad, you could always depend on him to rally round in a crisis.

'So what is it then?' asked Alan.

Maria didn't reply. So much had happened that it just didn't seem possible to tell him about it. Where could she begin?

Alan answered his own question. 'It's all right, I know. New house, new school next week. Everything must seem so weird.'

'You're telling me,' whispered Maria.

He didn't know the half of it, she thought. She'd encountered more weirdness since yesterday than in the rest of her life.

Alan sat down beside her on the bed. 'But if there is anything wrong, you can tell me. You know that, don't you? You can tell me anything.'

Maria looked at him. For a moment she was tempted – but it was still impossible. For the moment, anyway. Maybe when she'd sorted things out…

She put her arms round him and gave him a hug, burying her head in his shoulder.

Mrs Wormwood arched her back, smoothed the skin on her slender neck and adjusted her black silk dress at the collar. She felt awkward and uncomfortable, as if her skin didn't really fit. It always took a moment or two to get used to being back in human form.

She sat down behind her desk. 'Oh, it felt so good to be myself again. These clumsy human oxen…'

Davey was standing over Kelsey, looking down at her. She was stretched out on a couch, her eyes closed. He reached down and rolled back an eyelid, then straightened up.

'The girl's still unconscious. I'm surprised you didn't kill her.'

'These miniature versions have parents. And parents ask questions.'

Davey went over and sat in the chair before the desk. 'And what did we learn?'

Mrs Wormwood shuddered. 'The thoughts of a child are chaos!' She put her fingertips to her temples, accessing the information from Kelsey's jumble of a mind. 'Late homework. Is she fat? Will she ever be kissed? And she worships something called "The Holy Oak".' She paused. 'No… Hollyoaks! Her parents fight. She wishes she were younger, she wishes she were older. This world scares her, so very much…'

'What about Sarah Jane Smith?'

'Oh, she knows her. Bannerman Road, number thirteen. And yes! Miss Smith lives alone. No support, no defences.'

'Then I can attack?'

'Oh yes,' whispered Mrs Wormwood. 'Have some fun.' She rose and moved over to Kelsey. 'And I filleted the memories. This one will remember nothing.'

She snapped her fingers, and Kelsey opened her eyes. She blinked, confused.

'Oh, right…Hiya.' She struggled to sit up. 'I'm so shamed, I'm asleep in your office.'

Mrs Wormwood gave her a benevolent smile. 'We've looked after you. And don't worry, Davey can take you home.' She turned to Davey. 'Off you go, Bannerman Road. Enjoy!'

Davey smiled down at Kelsey and helped her to rise. He offered her his arm, and Kelsey, delighted, took it. They entered the lift and the door slid closed.

Smiling, Mrs Wormwood watched them go.

It wouldn't take Davey long to reach thirteen Bannerman Road. And once he did – there would be no more trouble from Sarah Jane Smith.

There would be no more Sarah Jane Smith.

Chapter Seven

Attack of the Bane

The boy sat on an over-stuffed sofa in the pleasant, rather old-fashioned sitting room of Sarah Jane's house. There were shelves of books, a brightly-coloured glass lampshade, comfortable armchairs and a scattering of assorted ornaments, including a carved wooden elephant.

The boy looked round the room with an expression of mild amazement. Like everything else, this was all totally new to him.

He rose politely as Sarah Jane came into the room. She was carrying a tea tray – cups of tea, sandwiches, slices of cake. She put the tray down on a little table and turned to the boy, continuing an earlier conversation.

'You must have a name. If I'm Sarah Jane then you're…?'

'All I know is, I had to run.'

Sarah Jane sat, gesturing to the boy to sit as well.

'But you can talk, someone must have taught you that. Who was it?'

'Everyone,' said the boy simply.

'What does that mean – "everyone"?'

'I am everyone. And then I had to run. The girl came, Maria, and then you.'

Sarah Jane sighed. She just didn't seem to be getting anywhere. Somehow she knew that the boy was being honest with her. She felt he didn't know the meaning of deceit. Yet his answers didn't make any kind of sense.

She persevered. 'Think back,' she urged. 'Before you ran, what can you remember?'

The boy's answer was as simple as it was baffling.

'I was born when I ran.'

'But you must have a home.'

The boy looked round the pleasant, comfortable room. 'Is this your home?' he asked.

'Yes, it is.'

'Can I live here?'

Sarah Jane stared at him for a moment and then smiled regretfully.

'No… No, I don't think so.'

The boy took a sandwich from the tray and studied it.

'Help yourself,' said Sarah Jane.

'Is this food?'

'Food and drink.'

'Which is which?'

Sarah Jane gave him a puzzled look. Before she could answer, a voice came from upstairs.

'Sarah Jane?'

It was a masculine voice, deep, calm and authoritative.

'Who's that?' asked the boy.

'No one,' said Sarah Jane hastily.

'There was a voice.'

'No, there wasn't!'

The voice came again, a little louder this time. 'Sarah Jane?'

Sarah Jane went to the sitting room door and yelled up the stairs. 'Not now!'

'I thought you lived alone,' said the boy.

Sarah Jane closed the door and put her back to it. 'I do. And whatever happens, you're not to go upstairs, have you got that? It's private. Don't ever go upstairs unless I say so.'

'You don't trust me,' said the boy.

There was no surprise or resentment in his voice. He was simply stating an observed fact.

Sarah Jane gave him a despairing look.

'I don't even know you,' she said.

She came across and sat down opposite the boy, flicked open her watch and held it up to his face. It gave off a rapid series of bleeps.

'Don't be afraid,' said Sarah Jane. She studied the data scrolling across the little screen. 'Not alien. A normal healthy lad. Human, ageing rate normal…' She stared at the screen as the data changed. 'But this says you were born 360 years ago.' She studied the little screen more closely. 'No. You were born 360 *minutes* ago.'

The boy smiled. 'Is that good or bad?'

A gleaming black saloon car pulled up and parked outside Sarah Jane's house.

Davey was behind the wheel, Kelsey beside him.

'Here we are, Bannerman Road,' said Davey. 'Off you go then.'

Kelsey gave him her most flirtatious grin. 'I don't

have to be home till six,' she said hopefully. 'We could go for a burger.'

'Get out,' snapped Davey. Then he smiled and fished an orange bottle from under the seat. 'And don't forget – drink Bubble Shock.'

Kelsey grinned, took the bottle, got out of the car and ran across the road. She was heading for Maria's house, but Davey neither knew nor cared.

He stared at Sarah Jane's house – and smiled again. But this time it was a very different sort of smile.

Maria sat despondently on the sofa in her sitting room.

Her father came back into the room. 'Here comes trouble.'

He stepped aside to reveal Kelsey, who went on the attack. 'Well, thanks for abandoning me. Some friend you are!'

'I'm making a snack,' said Alan hastily. 'Do you want some, Kelsey? Beans on toast.'

Kelsey shook her head. 'Too many carbohydrates.'

'Right, you can starve,' said Alan cheerfully, and went into the kitchen.

'Where were you?' asked Maria, keeping her

voice low. 'All the alarms went off and I was running round the factory looking for you.'

Kelsey's attention was elsewhere. 'He's all right, your dad, he's a bit fit.'

'Oh shut up!' said Maria impatiently. 'Where'd you get to? Just tell me Kelsey. The factory – what happened?'

Davey reached through the gap between hedge and gatepost and slipped the bolt on the back gate. He slipped into the back garden and moved around the back of Sarah Jane's big old house, looking for a way to get in undetected. He heard low voices from an open window and crept towards it…

Sarah Jane was staring at the boy, still wondering what to make of him. The boy, meanwhile, was flicking through a book he'd lifted from a shelf.

Sarah Jane registered what he was doing. 'You can read?'

'I can now.'

She stared at him. 'What? You just learnt?'

'It's easy! Just letters and words.'

Sarah Jane studied more data. 'Forgive me, but if you don't mind…could you just lift up your top? So I can see your stomach.'

'Okay,' said the boy. He lifted the bottom of his loose tunic, revealing a completely smooth stomach.

Sarah Jane stared at it in amazement.

'You've got no belly button!' said Sarah Jane.

'Is that good or bad?'

'I don't know – but everyone who's born has got a belly button.'

'Then why not me?'

'I'm sorry, but I don't think you were born. I think you were grown.'

Outside, Davey stiffened at the sound of her words. The woman knew too much – too much to live. He shimmered and began to *change*...

'And that's all I remember,' said Kelsey concluding her story. 'Waking up in her office. Honestly, I was mortified. And then they drove me home.'

'Hold on,' said Maria suddenly. 'Who drove you home?'

'The muffin,' said Kelsey.

'The guide? The man from the tour? He's here? On Bannerman Road?'

'Yeah, what about it?'

Horrified, Maria jumped up, running for the front door. 'Dad, I'm going out!'

Shaking her head, Kelsey followed.

They ran across the road and up the drive to Sarah Jane's front door.

Maria began hammering on the door. 'Open up, it's me! Maria!'

Kelsey stood back scowling. 'You are completely shaming me!'

Sarah Jane flung open the door. She looked very cross. 'I told you to leave me alone!' She tried to shut the door.

Maria shoved it open again.

'But it's the man from the factory, he's on the street, he's here –'

Then Kelsey gave an ear-splitting scream.

Sarah Jane and Maria turned. Halfway up the wall, something indescribably horrible was slithering around the side of the house towards them.

For a moment they stared, unable to believe what they were seeing.

In its true, natural form, the Bane looked something like a cross between a giant frog and an octopus. It was a good seven-feet long. Six enormous tentacles supported the shiny green globular body, three on each side. Their suckers clung easily to the brick of the house wall. A seventh tentacle formed a kind of tail. Smaller tentacles fluttered about its cavernous mouth, and in the centre of the bulbous head was one giant eye.

The Bane roared, a horrible slurping sound.

'Inside! Get in!' snapped Sarah Jane.

Maria and Kelsey dived into the house. Sarah Jane followed, slamming the door.

The door shuddered as the Bane hurled its weight against it.

Sarah Jane set her back to the door, struggling to keep it closed.

Kelsey went on screaming and babbling. *'What is that thing? What is it? That's not fair, what is it, what is it?'*

The boy strolled out from the sitting room.

'Hello, Maria, hello screaming girl.'

'Never mind hello,' said Maria. 'There's a great big alien out there!'

Outside, the Bane hurled itself against the door, roaring ferociously. The door shook, and started to splinter.

As the Bane thudded against the door, Sarah Jane heard the sound of the splintering wood and knew she couldn't hold the door shut much longer.

'Get upstairs!' she shouted.

The boy looked concerned. 'But we're not allowed.'

'I'm allowing you!' yelled Sarah Jane. 'Now go!'

'What is that thing?' shrieked Kelsey, for what seemed like the hundredth time.

'Just shut up and move,' snapped Maria. All three ran up the stairs.

Sarah Jane held on for a moment longer then abandoned the door and sprinted after them.

Outside, the Bane gave another savage roar. Gripping the door with its powerful front tentacles it ripped it from its hinges. Hurling the door aside, it scuttled into the house.

Slithering across the ceiling of the hall like a giant lizard, the Bane followed the retreating footsteps to the foot of the stairs, dropped to the floor and scuttled up after them.

Maria, Kelsey and the boy ran up one flight of stairs, then another, Sarah Jane close behind them. They came to a landing and Maria realised they'd reached the top of the house. There was nowhere else to go!

Roaring, the Bane slithered up the stairs after them.

They were trapped.

Chapter Eight

The weapon

Suddenly Kelsey saw a little door in the wall to the right. Before she could move, Sarah Jane came running up the stairs, pushed past them all, ran to the door and snatched it open.

'What's up there?' said Maria.

Sarah Jane turned in the doorway. 'No, you can't go up, I'll be ten seconds, just ten seconds…' She disappeared through the door.

Behind them they heard the slurping roar of the Bane as it clambered up the last few stairs. Ten seconds could be ten seconds too late, thought Kelsey.

The Bane's voice came floating up the staircase – a horribly distorted version of Davey's voice.

'You will die, Miss Smith, you and the squealing pigs.'

Kelsey huddled behind the other two for shelter. 'This is not happening,' she babbled. 'This is so not happening!'

'But that contradicts the facts,' said the boy logically.

He didn't seem frightened by what was happening, thought Maria. Just interested, the way he was interested in everything.

Now the Bane was at the top of the stairs, scanning them with its one great eye.

At the same time, Sarah Jane appeared in the doorway behind them. She was holding a silver-capped golden sphere with carrying handles, and a nozzle. There was some kind of firing stud on top of the sphere.

'First the children,' said the Bane in its horrible gloating voice. 'And then you, old woman.'

'Hey, not so much of the old!' said Sarah Jane, moving forward.

She held up the device with one hand and thumped the firing stud with the other. A jet of gas shot out, enveloping the Bane.

The effect was amazing.

Instantly, the Bane checked its advance, tentacles flailing. Then it shot backwards down the stairs and collapsed in a quivering heap on the next landing. It blurred and shimmered – and became Davey. But not the suave, polished, assured Davey they'd seen at the factory. This was a terrified, confused Davey. He stared up at Sarah Jane, eyes wide with fear.

'It's the muffin!' said Kelsey amazed.

The boy frowned. 'That is a muffin?'

Davey scrambled to his feet. He gave Sarah Jane one last fearful look and disappeared down the stairs.

All that remained of his alien monster form was a blob of thick black gunk on the spot where the Bane had transformed.

Sarah Jane shook the sphere and hit the firing stud. The gas jet expired with a final faint hiss.

'Pity,' said Sarah Jane, 'that was the last one.'

She went down to the landing below and Maria followed.

Neither of them noticed Kelsey, curious as ever, slipping through the door above, followed by the boy.

Kneeling down, Sarah Jane produced a pencil and prodded the black gunk.

Maria peered over her shoulder. 'What's going on?'

Sarah Jane gave her a warning look. 'Maria! Don't get involved.'

'I think it's a bit too late for that. And, thank you. You saved our lives.'

Sarah Jane smiled. 'I suppose I did.'

Maria smiled back, feeling, for the first time, that they might become friends.

Then Kelsey's voice came floating down from above. 'Oh my flipping heck!'

They looked up and saw that the landing above was empty and the door open wide. Maria turned and headed for the doorway.

'No, don't go up there!' shouted Sarah Jane. But it was too late.

Maria ran up to the next landing and through the open door. She climbed the short staircase and entered the room beyond to find Kelsey and the boy staring, awestruck – which wasn't surprising.

She was in a long attic room that ran the whole top floor of the big old house. Just beyond the doorway, three short steps led down to the main area.

It was a wonderful room, full of the most amazing things.

There were shelves running along the walls filled

with an untidy assortment of books and maps and charts. There was furniture, some, but not all of it antique – chairs and tables and sofas and armchairs. There was a battered computer on an old wooden desk. There were filing cabinets, some in gleaming metal, others in wood.

And then there were the machines and devices of all kinds scattered about the room. Some were on shelves or occasional tables or in display cases. Others were just shoved casually into corners and alcoves. Some were metallic and angular, like parts of robots or rocket engines. Others were glistening, organic, almost plant-like, as if they had been grown rather than manufactured. All were indescribably alien.

There were personal touches as well. Photographs, some framed, some stuck up here and there. One showed a fierce-looking Army officer with a clipped moustache, another a handsome square-jawed young man in a duffle coat. Sarah Jane's father and boyfriend, wondered Maria? There was a picture of a younger Sarah Jane, kneeling by what looked like a robot dog.

Despite its strange contents, the room was a friendly and welcoming place. Somehow it managed to be cluttered and cosy at the same time. It felt

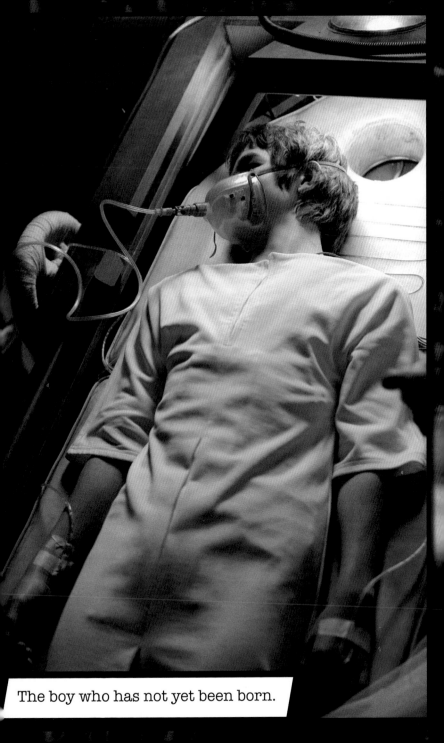

The boy who has not yet been born.

Davey tells Mrs Wormwood
there are children loose in
the Bubble Shock factory.

Mrs Wormwood admires
the creation of the Archetype.

Maria and the boy hide in the Ladies' toilets at the Bubble Shock factory.

Sarah Jane tells Maria of her adventures with the Doctor in the past.

Davey reports to Mrs Wormwood that he wasn't able to dispose of the children and Sarah Jane.

Maria and the boy are in awe of the objects in Sarah Jane's attic.

Sarah Jane tells them that alien life is invading Earth every day.

Kelsey decides to turn her attention from Sarah Jane's alien objects to the newborn boy.

Sarah Jane, Maria and the boy cower from the huge tentacles of the Bane Mother.

Maria and the boy crouch in front of the bus and the boy suddenly has an idea.

The boy destroys the Bane Mother with Sarah Jane's alien communicator.

warm and safe.

That was because the room *was* Sarah Jane, thought Maria. Her whole life was here...

Then a cross voice said, 'Who said you could all come up here? Don't touch anything.' And there was Sarah Jane in the doorway.

Maria was too curious to be scared. 'These things...are they alien?'

'Some of them, yes.'

'Where did you get them?'

Sarah Jane sighed. 'I suppose you've seen too much now. And it's not as if anyone's going to believe you. All right...'

She sat down on the room divider steps. Maria came and sat beside her.

'Aliens are falling to Earth all the time,' Sarah Jane went on. 'Not just those stories on the news, all sorts of creatures. Some have got lost – like the one you saw me sending home last night. Some of them crash-land – and some of them want to invade.' She looked hard at Maria. 'Do you still believe me?'

'Yes.'

'Really? How come?'

Maria considered. 'Because you're bonkers – but I don't think you're a liar.'

Sarah Jane smiled wryly. 'That's nice to know –

except for the bonkers bit.'

The boy had been quietly studying the room, unlike Kelsey, who had been wandering round picking things up and putting them down.

Suddenly he said, 'This place is beautiful.'

Sarah Jane was genuinely touched. 'Thank you.'

Kelsey picked up an old-fashioned magnifying glass and studied the boy through one magnified eye.

'You're not so bad yourself, fella!'

'What does that mean?'

Kelsey grinned wickedly. 'Oh, he's mine!'

The boy turned to Maria. 'Is that good or bad?'

'That's bad!' said Maria. 'That's very bad.'

Kelsey gave her a disgusted look.

Maria turned back to Sarah Jane and gestured around the room. 'All this…is it just you though? On your own?'

Sarah Jane rose from the step and paced about the room.

'The government knows all about aliens, and there are secret organisations dedicated to finding them. But they tend to go in with all guns blazing. I just think there's a better way of doing it.'

'But how did you get started?'

'I met this man,' said Sarah Jane. 'A very special

man, called the Doctor.' She gazed into space, her face radiant with memories. 'Years ago, we travelled together.'

'In space?' asked Maria.

Sarah Jane nodded. 'In space and time. Then it came to an end. Suddenly, I was back to a normal life. Electricity bills, burst pipes, bus tickets and rain…'

Kelsey had plonked herself into a seat in front of an astral telescope.

'She's completely loop-the-loop,' she announced.

Sarah Jane turned to Maria. 'You see? Who can I talk to about it? For years I tried to forget…' She wandered over to a chair near Maria and sat down. 'Then I met him again – the Doctor. We'd both changed, but it's funny – we were both still the same. I learnt that I could carry on, here on Earth, doing what we always did.' She gazed around the room. 'That's when I started this. I began my life again.'

Fascinating as all this was, Maria was more worried about the present.

'And the Bubble Shock factory…it's run by aliens?'

'Oh, right, everyone's an alien,' jeered Kelsey.

'You, me, the Pope, James Blunt…actually I can believe that one!'

'But Kelsey, you saw it,' protested Maria. 'That great big alien creature.'

'I saw a muffin in a suit,' said Kelsey defiantly. 'That's all! Like in films, it's all pretend!'

A high-pitched beeping began to fill the room. It seemed to come from a shuttered wooden cabinet on the wall.

Maria jumped. 'What's that?'

'Another invasion obviously,' muttered Kelsey. 'Little green men.'

Sarah Jane ran to the cabinet, separated the wooden shutters, one up, one down, to reveal a door of an old-fashioned safe.

'He's circled back again!' she said happily.

She spun the combination lock and pulled open the door to reveal a monitor screen.

Maria leaned forward to look. On the screen was a blazing vortex of fire, like a miniature sun. A scattering of rocks and asteroids orbited around it. Floating, suspended in the centre of it all, was a robot dog – the one in the picture on Sarah Jane's wall.

'There was a scientific project in Switzerland,' explained Sarah Jane. 'They created their own black hole. If it gets free the Earth would be swallowed up. K-9's sealing it off.'

Maria looked puzzled. 'K-9?'

'He's my friend,' said Sarah Jane, as if that explained everything.

Kelsey wandered over for a look. 'K-9 as in canine? That is so lame.'

'He's been in there for a year and a half now, plugging the distortion,' said Sarah Jane. 'Every so often he passes my way.'

Kelsey shook her head in disbelief. 'Your best friend is a metal dog with its bum stuck in a black hole?'

Sarah Jane nodded. 'I know!' She spoke into the screen. 'How are you K-9?' she said affectionately. 'How do you feel?'

The dog replied in a metallic robot voice. 'Misunderstanding of the nature of this unit, Mistress. I do not feel. However, all circuits are functioning at full capacity.'

Maria leaned forward. 'Can you ever come out, K-9?'

'Oh, K-9, this is Maria,' said Sarah Jane.

'Greetings, young mistress,' said K-9. 'I cannot emerge until this breach is sealed.'

'How long will that take?' asked Maria.

'I cannot estimate the duration of this task.'

'What does he eat, nuts and bolts?' scoffed Kelsey.

'The small female is hostile,' said K-9.

'Don't listen to her,' said Maria.

'Regret I must transfer my coordinates, Mistress,' announced K-9.

'Bye bye, K-9,' said Sarah Jane. 'Good dog!'

'Affection noted, Mistress,' said K-9 and faded away.

Sarah Jane closed the safe door and drew the shutters.

'How long's he gone for?' asked Maria.

'I don't know, but I miss him.'

Kelsey giggled.

Sarah Jane rounded on her fiercely. 'And don't you laugh, Kelsey Hooper. He was my dog, my daft little robot dog and I miss him. And now I'm on my own.'

She sank into a chair and looked wearily around her. The trouble was, she wasn't alone any more. Now she had three kids on her hands. And she still had to deal with the Bane.

She knew that Davey's defeat would only madden them. The Bane would never accept defeat. Not now, when she knew too much about them.

They were sure to attack again. The only questions
were when? And how…?

Chapter Nine

Takeover

One of the Bane was being dealt with already.

Looking scruffy and dishevelled, Davey stood before Miss Wormwood's desk.

He knew that he was doomed. The Law of the Bane did not tolerate failure. Yet, perhaps because he had spent so much time in human form, he couldn't resist trying to save himself.

'Forgive me,' he babbled. 'She had weapons, terrible weapons…'

'You know the penalty,' said Mrs Wormwood icily. 'A hunter who loses his prey is unfit to serve the Bane Mother.'

'I'll go back,' promised Davey. 'I'll go back and kill her!'

He knew, even as he spoke, it was useless.

He was appealing to the mercy of the Bane – and the Bane had no mercy.

'Kill her? I can manage that on my own,' said Mrs Wormwood.

Touching the jewel at her throat, she blurred and shimmered and reared up above him in her Bane form. Her tentacles reached out for him.

'Mother eats the children that fail her. You will become food!'

Jaws gaping wide, she swooped down.

Davey screamed.

Sarah Jane sat at a little laboratory table, studying a test tube holding some of the evil black glop the Bane attacker had left behind. She was subjecting it to a variety of tests. It always helped to know your enemy.

Maria sat close by her, watching intently. In the background, Kelsey and the boy wandered around the room, looking at things, picking them up and putting them down. Resigned to their presence by now, Sarah Jane ignored them.

Maria spotted a familiar object on a table and picked it up. It was a heart-shaped disc. It bore a little screen and it was studded with controls. Sarah Jane had been holding it the night Maria had seen her with the alien in her garden.

'What's this then?'

Sarah Jane looked up. 'Some sort of communicator. It was a gift, from the person you saw last night. She said if I ever needed help, I should use it to call her.'

Just what they needed, thought Maria. Help from some alien being, maybe with super powers.

'Then let's call her!'

Sarah Jane smiled. 'She meant help with poetry. She was a Star Poet from Arcateen Five. Not much use to us now – unless you want to rhyme "trouble" with "double".'

The boy wandered over. 'Let me see.'

Maria looked at Sarah Jane, who nodded briefly.

Maria handed the device to the boy. 'Be careful.'

The boy stood holding the device, turning it over and over in his hands.

Sarah Jane looked thoughtfully at him. 'He knows nothing about the world. Everything is new to him. I think he's some sort of experiment. Those aliens created him.'

'He's their child,' said Maria.

'He's still human,' said Sarah Jane.

She stood up, went over to the boy and took the device away from him.

'If you don't mind…I don't like people going through my things.'

She looked round for somewhere to put the device. Her coat was hanging over the back of a chair, and she shoved the disc into the pocket.

The boy accepted her decision with his usual calm. His curiosity remained unabated.

'That device on your wrist,' he said. 'It detects alien life?'

'That's right.'

'Then what's it detecting now?'

'How do you mean?' Sarah Jane looked at her watch. The hands were whirring round and it was beeping almost inaudibly. She flipped it open and studied the data on the little screen. 'He's right!'

Maria jumped up in alarm. 'There might be one of those alien things outside right now!'

'No wait a minute,' said Sarah Jane. Holding out the watch she swung it around the room. The beeping of the watch grew louder and louder and she followed the sound. It led her straight to Kelsey, who was slumped back on a couch, leafing through a comic.

Sarah Jane stood looking down at her, studying the device on her wrist.

Maria came hurrying over. 'Kelsey, you're an alien!'

'You wish!'

'No, it's not her,' said Sarah Jane.

There was a bottle of Bubble Shock on the couch beside Kelsey. Sarah Jane snatched it up.

'Oi, that's mine,' protested Kelsey.

Sarah Jane held her watch close to the bottle. The device beeped frantically, and data scrolled across the screen.

'It's the drink. It's that ingredient – Bane!'

'Well, it's organic,' said Kelsey uneasily.

'More than that,' said Sarah Jane. 'It's alive!' She peered at the little screen. 'Species identified – Bane. It's not just an ingredient, it's an alien. This is the secretion of…' She peered at the screen. 'Oh, I need glasses – the secretion of a Bane Mother.' She looked up. 'There's a piece of living Bane inside every bottle of Bubble Shock!'

'I've been drinking that stuff,' shrieked Kelsey indignantly. 'And it's alien!'

'Thought you didn't believe in aliens,' said Maria.

'Oh, you can shut up,' said Kelsey. 'I've got things from outer space in my stomach!' She looked up at Sarah Jane. 'What are you going to do about it?'

'It's not my fault!'

'Yeah?' said Kelsey furiously. 'You've got all this stuff, all these gadgets, you sit here talking all day, just yapping on about monsters and planets and things. What good is that? Why don't you actually do something?'

Sarah Jane glared at Kelsey then it struck her. Maybe, just maybe, Kelsey had a point. She forced herself to be calm.

'Right then, Kelsey. Just you watch.'

Sarah Jane looked across to the other side of the room and raised her voice.

'Mr Smith, I need you.'

'Yes, Sarah Jane,' said the deep masculine voice.

Two sections of wall slid back like hidden gates and the complex console of a giant computer emerged. The wall above it slid upwards, revealing a huge screen, a complicated symbol revolving at the centre.

'Mr Smith is a computer,' said Sarah Jane.

It was bigger, more elaborate than any computer Maria had ever seen or heard of, and now she knew why.

'An alien computer,' she whispered.

Sarah Jane addressed the computer like someone talking to an old and valued friend.

'Mr Smith, I want a direct visual link to Mrs Wormwood at the Bane factory. Can you get coordinates?'

'Accessing,' said the deep voice.

Maria was amazed. 'What, you can just phone her up?'

'Mr Smith can hack into anything,' said Sarah Jane confidently.

'But why do you want to talk to them?'

'Because I want to be fair,' said Sarah Jane.

It was something she'd learned from the Doctor. Even a savage invading alien species deserved one chance to make peace.

'Coordinates 177753957365549362874875969587476383940954-05-5,' said Mr Smith. As he spoke the numbers scrolled across the screen.

'That's like their phone number,' said Sarah Jane.

'Visual link connecting,' said Mr Smith.

Mrs Wormwood, now back in human form, was sitting at her office desk, digesting Davey, when the giant screen in her office came to life. On it appeared the face of Sarah Jane. Clearly, this annoying woman had access to some very advanced technology.

Mrs Wormwood stood up. 'Oh, very clever!'

'Mrs Wormwood,' said Sarah Jane. 'Thanks for all the assassination attempts.'

'My pleasure,' said Mrs Wormwood bitterly. 'The next one will involve harpoons!'

'I know who you are and what you are,' said Sarah Jane. 'Bane! Now, leave this planet.'

Mrs Wormwood seemed amused. 'Are you declaring war?'

Sarah Jane put everything into one heartfelt plea.

'Mrs Wormwood, the universe is huge, and Earth is so small. You don't need to do this. I'm asking you, as the representative of one species to another, just leave this world. Just leave us in peace – please!'

'And if I don't?'

'Then I shall have to do – something,' said Sarah Jane.

Even as she spoke, she knew it sounded pretty feeble.

Mrs Wormwood knew it, too.

'Very well,' she said. 'In the language of your young ones – bring it on!'

She picked up the remote and switched off the screen.

A little crestfallen, Sarah Jane said, 'That didn't go too well.'

'How are you gonna stop them?' asked Maria.

'You tell me!'

Maria was horrified. 'What? You mean you haven't got a plan? Nothing?'

'Nope,' said Sarah Jane cheerfully. 'The people I fight have plans and weapons, but I don't. That's what makes me different.'

It could also be what makes you dead, thought Maria.

Mrs Wormwood stood in the pipe room below the nest of the Bane Mother.

Her hands to her temples, she was concentrating furiously.

'Mother! Events have escalated. We must declare war on mankind.'

An angry roar came from above and the pipes shuddered.

The Bane Mother hated to be disturbed, to be asked to exert herself, but there was no alternative.

'Open your mind, Mother,' chanted Mrs Wormwood. 'You must convert the humans containing Bane. They will convert the rest.' She raised her arms in supplication. 'Let this become – Bane world!'

The central section of the roof slid open revealing

the giant green eye of the enormous Bane Mother, surrounded by undulating tendrils.

The great green eye closed for a moment and then opened again. But now the pupil glowed bright orange…

In the window of a trendy café in town, two girls sat drinking Bubble Shock. Suddenly, their expressions became fixed, frozen. A sickly orange glow, a kind of aura, flickered about their heads. Moving as one, they rose and left the café.

All over the town, indeed, all over the world, similar scenes were taking place. The disciples of the Bane, with Bane coursing through their systems, rose and obeyed the command of the Bane Mother. They had no choice.

In his kitchen Alan, Maria's dad, slammed down his bottle of Bubble Shock on the kitchen table. An orange glow flickered about his head. His face blank, his eyes fixed, he rose and strode from the house.

'Look at Kelsey Hooper! Look!' the boy shouted.

Sarah Jane and Maria turned.

Clutching her bottle of Bubble Shock, Kelsey

was staggering towards them. An orange glow flickered around her head. She slumped forward over a sofa.

'Help me…' she gasped.

'Oh God, it's beginning,' said Sarah Jane. 'Kelsey, fight it!'

It was too late for that. Kelsey straightened up, her face cold and hard. Holding out her bottle of Bubble Shock she stalked towards them. 'Drink it! Drink it!' she chanted.

'It's the Bane,' gasped Maria in horror. 'They're taking people over!'

Chapter Ten

Counter-attack

Sarah Jane's reaction was immediate. 'Out! Quickly! Out!'

Grabbing her jacket from the chair, she herded them out of the house.

Kelsey marched after them, holding out her bottle of Bubble Shock.

'Drink it!' she chanted. 'Drink it!'

The three of them ran from the house.

'Got to get to the factory!' said Sarah Jane determinedly, as they emerged into the street.

Maria was close behind her. 'I'm coming with you.'

'You're staying here!'

Maria looked across the road and saw her father coming out of their house. He was walking stiffly, like a zombie.

'Dad, stay indoors,' she shouted. 'There's all this stuff happening.'

Alan's face was expressionless, his eyes blank. He held out a bottle of Bubble Shock. 'Drink it!' he commanded.

Maria looked at him in horror. 'Dad, no…'

In the pipe room. Mrs Wormwood and a group of guards lifted their eyes reverently to the ceiling. The central roof section slid back, revealing the huge glowing eye of the Bane Mother. The gaping mouth roared, and tendrils flailed around it.

Mrs Wormwood raised her arms in supplication.

'Mother stirs!' she said ecstatically. 'Those who have not taken Bane must be converted.'

The rest of the roof slid back, revealing the massive writhing body of the Bane Mother. Great tentacles lashed and flailed about her.

Kelsey came out of the house and joined them. She stalked towards them, zombie-like, her eyes fixed, her face blank. She held out a bottle of Bubble

Shock. 'Drink it!' she commanded. 'Drink it!'

Alan marched across the road towards them, holding out his bottle of Bubble Shock.

'Drink it!'

Maria ran to her father.

'Dad, listen to me, don't…that's not you, it's that thing, it's the drink, it's the Bane…'

Alan ignored her. It was quite clear that he didn't recognise his daughter. She was just another subject for conversion.

'Drink it!'

Sarah Jane looked about her. Up and down the street, people were coming out of their houses. Holding out bottles of Bubble Shock they spread out like an army of zombies.

'Drink it!' they chanted. 'Drink it! Drink it!'

Sarah Jane grabbed Maria's arm. 'I'm sorry, we can't help them, the only thing we can do is get to the factory. Get in the car!'

She pushed Maria towards the car – the boy was already in the back seat – and they climbed in.

The crowd moved menacingly towards the car, Alan and Kelsey in the lead.

'Drink it! Drink it! Drink it!'

'This is bad,' said the boy from the back seat. 'I recognise bad.'

'What are we going to do?' wailed Maria.

'Maria, there are two types of people in the world,' said Sarah Jane. 'People who panic – and then there's us. Got that?'

'Got it!' said Maria bravely.

It was a tricky job, weaving the convertible through the crowd. Sarah Jane didn't want to run anyone over, and people made no attempt to get out of their way. Somehow she managed it and as soon as she reached a relatively clear area she picked up speed.

As they drove towards the factory the nightmare scene continued. First in quiet suburban avenues, then in the busy streets of the city centre, the blank-eyed disciples of Bubble Shock marched forwards, orange bottles held out.

'Drink it! Drink it! Drink it!'

The few people not under the Bubble Shock influence, the two per cent, reacted in panic, trying to flee the advancing mob. Many were seized and held by members of the crowd, while others poured Bubble Shock down their throats.

Faces loomed towards the car, mad eyes glaring, orange bottles thrust out.

Fanatical voices reached them inside the car. 'Drink it! Drink It! Drink it!'

Weaving and dodging, driving as fast as she could without killing anyone, Sarah Jane drove on.

Arms raised, Mrs Wormwood gazed upward at the writhing creature above her.

'Mother welcomes her new children. Come to us, newborn Bane. Come to us!'

In the streets around the factory the possessed disciples of the Bane began marching towards the Bane Mother.

Sarah Jane's car zoomed up to the locked factory gates. Without stopping she uncapped her sonic lipstick with her teeth, and held it out of the window. The gates swung open and the car drove through. The gates closed behind them.

Sarah Jane parked beside the Bubble Shock bus and they all jumped out.

'I'm going inside,' snapped Sarah Jane. 'You stay here.'

Maria shook her head. 'No way!'

They ran towards the main building.

Sarah Jane pointed her sonic lipstick at the main door. Nothing happened.

'They've got a deadlock seal!'

'What does that mean?' asked Maria.

'We can't get in!'

'Sarah Jane!' called the boy urgently.

They turned and saw that a growing crowd was gathering at the gates, moaning, chanting, holding out their bottles of Bubble Shock.

'Drink it! Drink it! Drink it!'

Maria turned to Sarah Jane. 'We can't go back and we can't get in. What do we do?'

Sarah Jane frowned in concentration. 'There's got to be a way of getting in, there's got to be. What do I do?' She spoke as if to some unseen companion. 'Oh, Doctor, help me! Come on, think!'

She looked all around, her eyes fixing on her car, and on the Bubble Shock bus.

'Oh yes!'

In the pipe room, Mrs Wormwood was addressing the guards, gloating over the future conquest of the Bane.

'All the humans who don't submit will be reduced to liquid. Then the Bane will drink them…'

She stiffened and turned round. 'What's that noise?'

She could hear the maddening jingle that accompanied the Bubble Shock commercial on television. It grew louder…louder…

The Bane bus crashed through the wall in a shower of debris, broken pipes, breeze blocks and brick-dust flying everywhere.

Mrs Wormwood staggered back, hands protecting her face. As the dust settled, she saw Sarah Jane at the wheel of the bus.

She glared up at her, furious. 'Miss Smith!'

Sarah Jane jumped down from the driver's cab. 'Not too late for the party?'

She advanced on Mrs Wormwood. 'I warned you to leave this planet.'

With an effort, Mrs Wormwood recovered her poise. She pointed upward.

'Have you met my mother?'

Sarah Jane looked up and recoiled as the huge eye of the Bane Mother glared down at her. As massive tentacle lashed down, Sarah Jane ducked and it missed her by inches.

Maria jumped down from the bus.

'Leave her alone!'

'I told you to stay on-board,' said Sarah Jane.

'Too late for that.'

The boy followed Maria from the bus.

Mrs Wormwood smiled evilly. 'Oh, you've brought us the Archetype.'

Even at this dangerous moment, Sarah Jane's

scientific curiosity was aroused.

'He's a living, thinking human being,' she said. 'And yet you created him. What for?'

Mrs Wormwood was happy to boast of the scientific genius of the Bane.

'He's an assembly of thousands of different humans,' she said. 'A montage, you might say. A collage. On every tour of the factory we'd scan the guests, all 10,000 of them. We fed the strengths and weaknesses of every one of them into him. The Archetype.'

The boy nodded, confirming her story. 'I am everyone.'

'But why?' asked Maria.

'Our little problem, the two per cent who wouldn't touch Bane. In time, the Archetype could tell us how to modify our product. But since we have advanced our plans, he is no longer needed.'

Mrs Wormwood touched the great jewelled ring on her finger and the boy collapsed with a gasp of pain.

'No!' shouted Maria.

She ran to the boy and crouched down beside him. He looked up at her, eyes flickering. 'I'm so cold…freezing.'

Sarah Jane took off her jacket and covered him.

'You can't do that to him, he's only a boy. Mrs Wormwood, I'm begging you, let him go.'

'Oh, that's so sweet,' said Mrs Wormwood. 'But he's dying, and soon you will join him. Like all our enemies. Our slave control is activated all over the world.' Mrs Wormwood's eyes gleamed. 'The Time of Man is over. The Time of Bane has come!'

In all the streets around the factory, in streets all over the world, shuffling chanting crowds held out bottles of Bubble Shock and hunted down those still unconverted, forcing the orange liquid down their throats.

'Drink it! Drink it! Drink it!'

Humanity was enslaved.

Chapter Eleven

Victory

In the half-wrecked pipe room, the air filled with smoke and dust and steam, Mrs Wormwood was exulting in her final victory. The time of the Bane had come, and her only significant enemies had delivered themselves into her hands.

'You've failed, Miss Smith. This is where your lonely life has led you – to despair!'

'Except she's not alone,' said Maria. She straightened up. 'She's got me – and I've got this!' She held out her mobile phone and switched it on.

From high above, the Bane Mother twitched and roared.

Mrs Wormwood winced, but she was still smiling. 'The device is tiny. An irritation, that's all.

And now you've angered the Bane Mother. Do you really think that was wise?'

An enormous tentacle swooped down from the roof, snatched up a massive length of broken piping like a club, and swung it at Sarah Jane and Maria. They threw themselves down by the boy, and the great metal pipe missed them by inches.

'I told you to stay away from me,' said Sarah Jane as they crouched down.

Even in this moment of terrible danger, Maria knew that she wouldn't want to be anywhere else but at Sarah Jane's side.

'Know what?' she whispered. 'I'm still glad I didn't.'

Somehow she felt that things would still work out, that they'd defeat the Bane and win in the end.

At the moment, it didn't seem very likely.

Mrs Wormwood raised her arms in a frenzy of exultation.

'Descend, Bane Mother, and consume them!'

More giant tentacles descended as the huge monster above them began to move. The massive body heaved and writhed as it strove to leave the confinement of the nest.

Maria remembered the horror that had been the

transformed Davey. What could they do against a monster ten times the size?

Gathering all his strength, the boy struggled to a sitting position. He reached into the pocket of the jacket around his shoulders – Sarah Jane's jacket.

'You forgot this.'

He held up a heart-shaped device studded with controls.

Mrs Wormwood said contemptuously, 'And what is that?'

The boy fought to rally his failing strength.

'A signal device from another world.'

Mrs Wormwood stared at him.

'And what of it?'

'It's like a mobile phone. But to call across the stars it must be a million times more powerful.'

'Then it's a good thing you don't know our frequency,' said Mrs Wormwood. Only if the device was tuned to exactly the right frequency, could it do the Bane any real harm.

The boy looked at Sarah Jane. 'Mr Smith said it out loud.'

'But that was dozens of numbers,' she said.

'And I remember them.' He looked up at Mrs Wormwood. 'You gave me the memory of 10,000 humans.'

'Stop him!' screamed Mrs Wormwood.

Guards moved towards them, but the boy's fingers were flickering over the controls at incredible speed. He recited a string of numbers.

'Coordinates 17775395736554936287487596 9587476383940954-05-5.'

With one final effort, he summoned up the last of his strength and raised the alien communicator.

'Calling the Bane!'

He pressed the call button.

The result was spectacular.

A high-pitched whine filled the air and the Bane Mother roared in pain and recoiled. The great flailing tentacles withdrew at once and the huge bulbous body writhed in agony as the monster tried to retreat into the safety of its nest.

Mrs Wormwood clutched her temples in pain, as did the surrounding guards. Even Maria clapped her hands over her ears to block out the piercing howl.

'The Bane Mother,' screamed Mrs Wormwood. 'You're killing her!' She pointed a commanding finger at the boy. 'Archetype! I order you to stop!'

Holding out the alien device, the boy ignored her command.

'You've made him human,' shouted Sarah Jane.

'He's ours!' She turned to Maria. 'Come on, give me a hand.'

They helped the boy to his feet. Supporting him between them, they fled from the noise and chaos of the pipe room.

Powerless to stop them, Mrs Wormwood staggered, hands clutching her temples. High above them the massive form of the Bane Mother writhed and roared...

Sarah Jane, Maria and the boy emerged into a dark corridor. All around them lights flashed, alarms rang and steam gushed from broken pipes.

'Come on,' cried Sarah Jane, and led them in the direction that she desperately hoped led to the exit.

Mrs Wormwood, still clutching her temples, staggered from the pipe room and stumbled into the corridor. She saw a staircase ahead of her and felt her way blindly up it, hoping to reach the open air...

The three fugitives came to a side door. To their relief, it led to the open courtyard and they began running towards Sarah Jane's car.

Mrs Wormwood saw daylight at the end of a corridor and ran towards it, only to find her way barred by a metal grille. Through it she could see Sarah Jane, Maria and the Archetype as they ran from the factory.

'Until the next time, Miss Smith!' she screamed.

Sarah Jane and Maria, supporting the boy between them, were still running when the blast of a mighty explosion sent them staggering. They turned. Behind them most of the factory had exploded in a sheet of flame. Smoke filled the air and flaming debris rained down.

Stunned and delighted, they stared at the smoking ruins. They looked at each other and began laughing in almost hysterical relief

'We stopped them,' said Maria.

Sarah Jane looked at the boy, who was standing up by himself, smiling.

'Are you all right?'

'Their control has gone,' said the boy. 'I'm free, and that's – good!'

'Oh yes,' said Sarah Jane. 'That's good!' She hugged him. 'I'd be dead without you. We all would. You're amazing!' She reached out to draw Maria into the embrace. 'The pair of you – amazing!'

'This is happiness, yes?' said the boy.

'Oh, yes,' said Sarah Jane. 'We did it!'

'We did it!' said Maria.

'We did it!' echoed the boy.

Linked in a group hug they spun round and round, laughing like idiots in happiness and relief.

Alan sat in his living room watching the news on television.

On the screen a pretty young newscaster, standing, for some reason, in front of the Houses of Parliament, was reporting on recent events. It appeared that extraordinary things had been going on all over the world, though as yet there was no satisfactory explanation.

'The Government has refused to comment,' said the newscaster, 'but stocks of Bubble Shock have been withdrawn from the shelves. The mass hysteria of this afternoon is being put down to a chemical imbalance of the brain...'

Alan shrugged and switched off the set, just as Maria shot into the room.

'Dad!' she shrieked and hurled herself into his arms, hugging him.

He patted her on the back. 'What's brought this on?'

She looked up and studied him. He seemed perfectly okay, very much his old placid self.

Maria hugged him again. 'I thought I'd lost you!'

Alan looked embarrassed. His recollection of recent events was hazy to say the least, and he had an uneasy feeling that he'd been doing some very strange things. But, like most people, he'd worked out an explanation that satisfied him.

'Oh, I had a bit of a turn, that's all. It's all over the news. They said some chemicals escaped from the Bubble Shock factory, gave everyone hallucinations...'

He looked up as Sarah Jane and the boy came into the room.

'Hello there.'

Sarah Jane studied him carefully for a moment. Like Maria, she was relieved to see that Alan, at least, seemed to have made a full recovery. With the Bane destroyed, perhaps everyone else would, too.

'Hello,' she said, a little awkwardly. 'Just checking everything's all right.'

'That's very neighbourly,' said Alan dryly, remembering their first meeting.

Sarah Jane smiled. 'Yes, well, sorry about before.' She held out her hand. 'Welcome to the neighbourhood.' They shook hands.

'It's certainly been lively,' said Alan. 'Is it always like this?'

Sarah Jane looked at Maria and smiled. 'No, this is a quiet day.'

Alan nodded towards the boy. 'And who's this?'

For a moment Sarah Jane was baffled. Who was the boy? What could she possibly say about him? She looked at Maria who looked anxiously back.

The boy looked anxious too. Sarah Jane and Maria were his only friends in this strange new world. What was his place? Did he even have one?

'This is…I suppose…this is my son,' Sarah Jane heard herself saying. 'My adopted son.'

The boy looked pleased, and Maria beamed.

'Hello,' said the boy politely.

He was filled with a vast relief. He knew who he was now. He was Sarah Jane's adopted son.

Alan held out his hand and they shook hands.

'And what's your name?'

Sarah Jane and Maria looked at each other. Another little problem they'd failed to think of.

'I don't have a name,' said the boy with his usual devastating frankness.

Alan looked baffled, and Sarah Jane tried to save the situation.

'Sorry,' she said hastily. 'Old family joke. He's called…'

But then – what was he called?

Before Sarah Jane could think of a name Chrissie burst into the room – full of herself and her own affairs as always. She looked reproachfully at Alan, putting him in the wrong as usual.

'Look at you, leaving your front door open, after everything that's happened! Did you hear about the chemicals? Oh, it was a nightmare.'

She went over to Maria, gave her a quick kiss, and carried on talking.

'I had Ivan chasing me round the bedroom saying, "Drink it! Drink it!" I said get off, but he wasn't having it.'

It occurred to Maria that perhaps her anti-Bane genes were inherited. It seemed Chrissie was in the two per cent as well.

'Haven't you finished unpacking yet, Alan?' Chrissie went on. 'You know what I said, the longer it stays in boxes the less it feels like a home…' She suddenly noticed Sarah Jane. 'And you are?'

'Sarah Jane Smith. I'm from over the road.'

'This is my mother,' said Maria, trying not to sound apologetic.

Chrissie stared at the boy. 'What's he wearing?'

'These are the clothes I was born in.'

'Right,' said Chrissie baffled. She turned back to Sarah Jane. 'Well, thanks very much, but, if you don't mind, I've had a bit of a trauma. Family time. Thanks for calling in.'

Sarah Jane accepted the dismissal politely. 'Okay, we'll be off.'

The boy studied Chrissie. 'This woman is rude.'

'Yes, we're definitely going,' said Sarah Jane brightly. She grabbed the boy's hand. 'Let's go home.'

'You don't have to go,' said Maria in embarrassment.

In a perfectly audible aside, Chrissie said, 'Come on now, Maria, invite the neighbours round and you never get rid of them. Next thing you know, it's holidays together, and that's a recipe for disaster.' She smiled at Sarah Jane insincerely. 'No offence, nice to meet you Sarah…Lou.'

Sarah Jane gave Maria a sympathetic smile.

'See you,' she said.

Maria watched them go as Chrissie rattled on.

'So, there he was, chasing me round the bedroom with a bottle of pop. I said, "That's novel!" Next thing you know, next door's doing the same thing! "Have you two been colluding?" I said. "When did that happen?"' Chrissie paused to draw breath and then changed the subject. 'Oh, and while I'm here, I'll have that cheque, thanks.'

Alan looked embarrassed. 'Give it a week, I've got to pay the removal men.'

'Well then, you should have planned,' said Chrissie crossly. 'That's you all over, Alan, no plans. Ivan's booked this villa outside Skiathos and it's gorgeous, he's put the deposit down but we've still got to pay the rest…'

Maria listened as Chrissie went on – and on. This was normal life, she supposed. Normal family life…

She thought about the amazing events of the last two days, and it suddenly struck her that she had another family now.

She smiled to herself, and slipped away.

Nobody noticed.

Chapter Twelve

Aftermath

It was night-time, a beautiful starry summer night, and Maria was sitting at a picnic table in Sarah Jane's garden. The garden where she had seen Sarah Jane and the alien Star Poetess. The place where it had all begun.

Sarah Jane came out of the house with a tray bearing a jug of lemonade and some glasses. She put the tray on the table, sat down and poured two glasses, handing one to Maria.

Sarah Jane held up her glass. 'Cheers…'

'Cheers! And it's normal pop!'

'Hooray for normal pop,' said Sarah Jane. A thought struck her. 'How's your friend Kelsey?'

Maria grinned. 'She's backtracking like mad,

saying it was all hallucinations. No such thing as aliens.'

'But we know better?' said Sarah Jane.

They exchanged a secret smile.

The boy came into the garden. They'd all been shopping that afternoon. Now he wore a grey T-shirt, a green fleece, brown jeans and trainers.

He looked like any other teenager, thought Maria.

'Oh, that's more like it,' she said.

The boy looked down at his new clothes. 'This is good?'

'Yep,' said Maria.

The boy went and sat by Sarah Jane and she gave him a glass of lemonade.

'How are you going to adopt him then?' asked Maria. 'I mean, you'll need forms and things. Who are you going to say his real mum is? The Bane Mother?'

'Mr Smith's sorted that one out.' Sarah Jane produced a sheaf of official-looking documents from her shoulder bag. 'All officially done and dusted. All he needs now is a name.'

Maria grinned at the boy. 'You can choose your own! What do you think?'

'I like yours, Maria.'

She shook her head. 'Maybe not…How about Jack? Josh? Nathan?'

'Harry? Alistair?' said Sarah Jane, remembering old friends. Then, in a completely different tone, she said 'Or – Luke?'

'Muffin?' said the boy.

Maria and Sarah Jane shook their heads.

'I like Luke,' said Maria thoughtfully.

'I like Luke,' said Sarah Jane.

'If you like Luke, I like Luke,' said the boy.

Sarah Jane paused for a moment.

'That's the name I was going to choose if ever I had kids,' she said, a little sadly. 'Except it never happened.'

'But now it has,' said Maria. 'Luke Smith. You're a mum!'

Sarah Jane smiled. 'I am!' She reached out and took Luke's hand.

Maria risked a more personal question. 'I never asked. Have you got a boyfriend or…'

'There was only ever one man for me,' said Sarah Jane. 'After him, nothing compared.' She paused for a moment, staring into space – or into the past. 'When I was your age I thought, oh, when I'm grown up, I'll know what I want, I'll be sorted. But you never really know what you want. You never feel grown up, not really, you never sort it all out. So, I thought I can handle life on my own. But after today…' She looked from Maria to Luke and smiled. 'After today, I don't want to!'

Luke was staring up at the sky, following a blinking light as it moved across the heavens.

'What's that?'

Maria looked. 'Just a plane.'

'That's a flying machine, right?'

'Or perhaps it's a spaceship,' said Sarah Jane. She looked up at the stars. 'I saw amazing things, out there in space. But there's strangeness to be found wherever you turn. Life on Earth can be an adventure too. You just need to know where to look.'

They sat, all three of them, staring up at the stars.

Three people, three friends, with a world of adventure before them.

If life on earth with Sarah Jane is an adventure then try travelling in time with the Doctor!

Decide your destiny by choosing the direction the story will go....

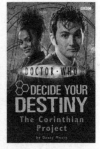

Eight titles to collect with four new books publishing in March 2008

Available from all good bookshops and www.penguin.co.uk